The Espressologist

A novel by

KRISTINA SPRINGER

To Athens, my first ever
Espressology match

SQUARE
FISH
An Imprint of Macmillan

THE ESPRESSOLOGIST. Copyright © 2009 by Kristina Springer. All rights reserved.
Distributed in Canada by H.B. Fenn and Company Ltd. Printed in December 2010 in
the United States of America by R. R. Donnelley & Sons Company, Harrisonburg, Virginia.
For information, address Square Fish, 175 Fifth Avenue, New York, NY 10010.

Square Fish and the Square Fish logo are trademarks of Macmillan
and are used by Farrar Straus Giroux under license from Macmillan.

Library of Congress Cataloging-in-Publication Data
Springer, Kristina.
    The Espressologist / Kristina Springer.
        p.   cm.
    Summary: While working part-time as a barista in a Chicago coffee bar, high school senior
Jane dabbles in matchmaking after observing the coffee preferences of her customers.
    ISBN: 978-0-312-65923-3
    [1. Coffeehouses—Fiction.   2. Dating services—Fiction.   3. Chicago (Ill.)—Fiction.]
I. Title.

PZ7.S7684575Es 2009
[Fic]—dc22

                                                                    2008016797

Originally published in the United States by Farrar Straus Giroux
First Square Fish Edition: January 2011
Square Fish logo designed by Filomena Tuosto
Book design by Irene Metaxatos
www.squarefishbooks.com

10 9 8 7 6 5 4 3 2 1

LEXILE HL640L

The Espressologist

1

Large Nonfat Four-shot Caffe Latte

*Cocky sex-deprived butthead guy drink. Expect only the utmost
stupidity to come out of his mouth. So-so body, could stand to
work out more. Crappy dresser. Dramatically stares at a woman
who comes in with a boob job. He looks like he is going to hurt
himself in the contortions he is twisting into . . .*

"Excuse me," the customer says, stepping up to the
counter. I quickly stop scribbling in my notebook and slide it
onto the shelf under the espresso machine.

"Sorry about that, sir. How can I help you?" I reply in my
most superefficient Wired Joe's barista voice.

"Jane, is it?" he says, reading my name tag and thinking he
is ever so personable and charming for calling me by name.

"I'd like a large nonfat four-shot caffe latte." I smile to myself. God, I'm good. It's getting to the point where I can guess most customers' drinks on sight. I grab a large white paper cup, write an NF in the milk box, and a 4 in the shots box, and set the cup down on the gleaming silver table for Sarah, the other barista working the counter, to start making the drink. I type the order into the cash register and look back up.

"That will be four eighty-five," I reply with a fake smile.

"Here's a five," he says. "Keep the change." Cha-ching! That will so help my college savings fund.

"Thank you, sir. Your order will be up in just a moment." The man heads over to the pick-up counter and positions himself to continue his study of Boob Job woman. Sarah draws the first of the four shots of espresso and dumps it into the waiting cup.

"What are you always writing in that notebook?" she whispers. I glance at her and stick up my index finger, indicating I'll tell her in a minute, after the customer has left the counter. Sarah tops off the espresso with freshly steamed milk and a dollop of foam.

"Large nonfat four-shot caffe latte," she calls out, even though the man is standing two feet away from her. It's just something we have to do. Corporate policy. He briefly breaks his gaze from Boob Job woman to look at Sarah and grab his drink. Do these kinds of guys even know what they look like? The man slinks away from the counter and settles into one of the big comfy blue velvet chairs and continues to stare. Oh

4

geez, he's going to make this woman get up and leave. A few seconds later she does, and he gives her a wink.

"So, what are you writing in there?" Sarah repeats.

"Nothing much. Just some notes. You could say I'm conducting my own field research."

"On what?"

"Well, people. Just people," I say. "Honestly it's nothing. Just something I like to do."

"Is it for school or something?"

Um . . . no. One would have to go to school to get assignments, right? I'm a senior at Lincoln High and done with all my core curriculum already. So it's a fluffy schedule for me this semester—we're talking ceramics, study hall, and home ec here. Well, except for the two college-credit courses I'm taking over at Anthony Carter Community College in the afternoons. But I haven't been there lately either—hey, I'm an equal opportunity ditcher. I've already applied to my DC (dream college) and I'm just waiting to hear from early admissions. It's not like I NEED to go to school. Whereas I NEED to work. With no scholarship prospects and no apparent college fund from Mom and Dad, I'll be footing my tuition bill next year. That's another thing: Mom and Dad don't know I've been ditching. And, crossing my fingers, they won't find out. They are both very career-oriented these days and trust me to do the right thing, and I do. Most of the time. And it helps that I've been able to sign my mom's name to school forms since the fifth grade.

"No, it's not for school," I say, purposely not telling Sarah that I haven't actually been to many classes in the last week or so. "Like I said, it's just something I've been doing."

"Well, don't let Derek catch you," she replies. I glance around the store but don't see Derek lingering anywhere.

It's not that I dislike our manager or anything—it's just that he's always mad about something or other. "What's his mood like today—pissy, extra pissy, or über-pissy?"

Sarah laughs. "I'd say just extra pissy."

"Oh fun. Any particular reason?" I ask.

"Todd again," she says, and rolls her eyes. As in Todd Stone, the hottie manager of the Wired Joe's two blocks west of us and Derek's direct competition. Todd's store is continually pulling in higher sales than ours and it just *kills* Derek. And then he takes it out on us.

"Where is he, anyway?" I ask, surprised he hasn't checked on us yet.

"In the break room scolding Em for something—I'm not sure what," Sarah tells me.

"Ooh. Em is here already? I didn't think she started until four-thirty." I immediately brighten. Em, short for Emily, has been my best friend since the sixth grade, when I farted really loudly in a stall in the girls' bathroom. Two of the popular girls were in there doing their makeup and said, "Ew . . . like . . . who is in there?" I stupidly answered, "Um . . . Jane Turner." They started laughing hysterically and I thought I'd die right there on the spot. Em was also in the bathroom washing her hands and told them, "At least that is temporary—you two smell like butt all the time." The girls responded with one of those "uh! I can't believe you just said that to me" sounds and left the bathroom. I peeked out the crack of the stall door and Em smiled at me in the mirror. We've been inseparable ever since (even though I was known as "Stinky Jane" for the rest of the school year).

"Yeah," Sarah says. "I guess Derek told her to come in early so he could talk to her. She looked a little scared."

"Scared? I doubt it," I disagree. I swear, nothing scares Em. She is the toughest chick I know. But now I'm a little worried. She CANNOT get fired. Working with her every day is one of the perks of the job. That and the free coffee.

"She's been back there awhile," Sarah replies. "I wonder what they are talking about."

"I'm sure it's nothing bad," I say, more to reassure myself than Sarah.

"You're probably right," she says. "Hey, it's pretty quiet in here." A guy who looks to be in his forties is sitting in the corner of the store reading a James Patterson book and sipping a white chocolate mocha, and a girl, most likely a college student, is at a table working on her laptop and drinking an iced caramel macchiato. "If you don't mind, I'm going to take my break." Sarah pulls out her cell phone and heads for the door.

"Sure, no problem." I turn to the sink and busy myself washing some of the dishes that have stacked up. When I turn around to reach for one of the large cookie trays I see *her*. The girl at the very top of my "People I Really Hope I Never See Again" list. Oh crap. With a freaking Wired Joe's on every corner in the city, why does SHE have to come into MINE? The glass door flies open and I'm smacked in the face with the cool November breeze.

Okay, calm down. Think fast. Where to hide? Behind the coffee-bean display? No, not enough room. Pull my blue apron over my head? Ick, there are some used coffee grounds smeared in the corner. Oh god, she is walking straight toward me. I'll just crouch down like I'm cleaning the floor and Sarah can help her. I sit fire-drill style behind the counter and wait.

Shoot. Sarah went outside, didn't she?

"Um . . . hello?"

Ugh. It's too late; she sees me. Melissa freaking Stillwell. Otherwise known as Meliss the Priss. Okay, so I'm the only one who calls her that. And only behind her back, of course, but that is beside the point. She's here now and I *so* don't want to talk to her. I pull chunks of my wavy brown hair out of the clip that is restraining it and muss them in front of my eyes, hoping she won't recognize me. There. It won't be so bad. I probably even look good this way.

"Sorry," I say as I straighten up. "What can I get for you?"

"Let's see," Melissa says, standing back so she can look at the menu overhead. I just now notice that she has a sidekick with her. Actually it's the same sidekick who always followed her around school last year. She's much shorter and not as pretty—almost invisible really, next to the great Melissa Stillwell. "What do you think, Gin?"

Ginny Davis looks up at the menu and shrugs. "Maybe frappycaps?"

"Uh, no," Melissa says sharply. "I'm doing South Beach this week so I can't have sugar."

Ginny sighs.

Small nonfat latte, I think to myself, and wait with my hand hovering over the keypad of the register.

"Okay, we'll have small nonfat lattes," Melissa decides.

Ha! I'm dead-on again.

"I'm sorry, was something funny about that?" Melissa looks pointedly at me with eyebrows raised and arms crossed, ready to do battle.

Whoops. Did I "Ha!" out loud?

"No, of course not," I say. "Just clearing my throat. So that's two small nonfat lattes, then?"

"Yeah, that sounds good." Melissa nods and flicks a platinum credit card across the counter to me with one cotton-candy-pink fingernail. Just then Ginny breaks into a huge smile. I can see the look of recognition in her eyes. Darn, darn, darn. Melissa looks at Ginny quizzically. "What are you smiling at?" she asks her. I move to the espresso station and grab two small white paper coffee cups with the famous Wired Joe's logo and mark them both with the drink order.

Just keep busy, don't even look at them. I give a sideways glance in their direction and see Ginny whispering in Melissa's ear. Melissa turns to look at me and breaks into a huge grin.

"Cousin Dater, is that you?" she asks.

ରେ୨ର

Melissa Stillwell ruined my entire junior year when she nicknamed me Cousin Dater. I had only just started getting over it this past summer after she graduated and I thought I'd never have to see her again. It happened at the homecoming dance. I had never gone to a high school dance before and my mom was all over me to go to this one. "You'll regret it years from now if you don't go," she said. "You'll look back at your high school yearbook and wish you had those memories." Yeah, right. Wishing for memories would have been more fun than being stuck with the ones I've got.

I had never been good with guys, so my mom suggested I take my über-hot cousin Nathan. Of course I didn't want to at first (I mean, ew . . . gross, he's my cousin!) but she convinced me that no one would ever know, and Nathan was so incredibly good-looking and so popular at his school that it would totally boost my reputation. After a few weeks of going back and forth with her, I finally agreed.

The dance started out just fine. I could totally tell that people were impressed with my date. But then stupid, selfish Nathan couldn't keep with the plan. I went into the bathroom to fix my makeup and when I came out I saw Nathan totally hitting on Melissa in front of the soda machine. I ran over to him, looped his arm with mine, and tried to yank him away but he wasn't budging. Melissa said, "Is this your date?" and Nathan replied, "Not really, I'm just doing a favor for my mom. This is my cousin Jane." Well, that was that. Melissa nicknamed me "Cousin Dater" and made sure that everyone in attendance at the Lincoln High homecoming dance knew that I was there with my cousin. I was MORTIFIED. Nathan left with Melissa and I had to find a ride home.

The nickname, unfortunately, caught on. Soon people I had never even met were calling me "Cousin Dater." My mom said, "Don't worry. It'll blow over. There will be a new drama with someone else next week and they'll forget all about you." Yeah. I inadvertently ticked Melissa off a week later and my destiny was sealed. We were in the same Spanish class and the teacher told me to ask Melissa for a pen in *español*. I somehow mistranslated and ended up calling her a pig. The whole class laughed and I knew I was doomed. Never piss off the pretty people.

"It IS you, isn't it?" Melissa asks again.

I hand her back her credit card. "I don't know what you are talking about."

"Oh, come on, you're the girl who took her hottie cousin to the Lincoln High homecoming last year. What was his name again?" She looks at Ginny. "Ethan or something, right? I went on a date with him. Terrible kisser." She flares her nostrils in disgust at the memory. I busy myself making the two lattes. Where are Sarah and Em? Why couldn't one of them make Melissa's blasted coffees? I stare straight ahead at the espresso machine and draw the first shot. I can feel tears starting to sting my eyes. Do NOT cry! The two girls move over to the counter to get in a better position to taunt me.

"So, Jane Turner, isn't it?" Melissa asks. "Still dating family members, Jane?" Both girls laugh.

I grab the cream instead of the skim milk and pour it into the foaming pitcher. There we go—we'll see who's laughing when she gets on the scale later.

"Ah, seriously, all kidding aside. What are you doing with yourself, Jane? You are a senior this year, right? Or did you drop out of high school to be a coffee girl?" Melissa smiles.

"I'm a barista," I nearly whisper.

"I'm sorry, what's that?" she says.

"A barista," I reply louder, "not a 'coffee girl.' " Melissa and Ginny both laugh even harder. Just then Em comes up behind me.

"What's so funny?" she asks, immediately recognizing both girls.

"Jane . . ." Melissa sputters. "She's . . . just so funny."

"Well, it looks like your drinks are ready," Em says curtly.

"Yeah, yeah, keep your apron on." Melissa glares at Em before turning to address me. "Looks like we'll be seeing you often, Jane. Ginny and I are going to the School of the Art Institute of Chicago just up the street. It's a top fashion school."

"I know." I try to act unimpressed when secretly I totally am. That's the school I'm waiting to hear from. I've wanted to study fashion there for as long as I can remember, way before all of the fashion reality TV shows made it supercool for everyone and their sister to study fashion. And Melissa's at *my* DC. I feel sick.

"Where did you say you want to go to school again?" Melissa asks.

"I didn't. Have a nice day," I tell her. I grab a rag and begin to clean the back counter. I hear the girls giggle as they leave the store. I pull out my notebook from underneath the espresso machine and quickly write:

Small Nonfat Latte
Bitch.

"What was that about?" Em asks once the girls are gone. "And what's with your hair?"

"Oh." I let down my hair and then pin it back up again, neatly this time, with the clip. "It was my disguise. Not like it worked or anything. As for Melissa and Ginny—I don't know. I guess they didn't have enough time torturing me last year, so they thought they'd follow me throughout life."

"You shouldn't put up with their crap, Jane."

"I know. But forget about them. What happened with Derek? You aren't in trouble, are you?"

"In trouble? Why would you think that?"

"Sarah thought you looked scared when you came in," I tell her.

Em laughs. "Scared, no. Irritated, yes. I hate coming in early. Especially when I'm not getting paid for it. And I had wanted to get some studying done before work." Em is taking advanced everything. She wants to be prelaw at DePaul University next year and she's very serious about keeping up her 3.8 GPA. I pull out a box of whipped cream lids from a cabinet to restock up front.

"So what did Derek want, then?" I ask.

"Oh, you're not going to believe this. He wants me to be the assistant manager! Like I have any bloody time to be the assistant manager!" Em is not British, but adopts a British accent whenever she gets really mad. It started shortly after we saw *Bridget Jones's Diary*.

"Really? That's kind of neat." I wonder why he didn't ask me. I have nothing but time. Not to mention I've been working here longer than Em.

"Well, I told him no," she says. "The extra two dollars an hour is not worth the headaches."

Raise? I could use a raise. "Hey, are you okay up here for a minute?"

"Sure. Where are you going?"

"To talk to Derek," I say, and give her a wink. Time to make things happen.

2

All right, ladies, stop your yapping and listen up," Derek says as he approaches the coffee counter. Ever the charmer, that one is. Sarah and Em both glare at Derek, arms folded across their chests. Derek is a mid-thirties *American Rock Star* contestant wannabe (seriously . . . he tried out and didn't make it on the show), with a shaved head, tat sleeves, and the beginnings of a beer belly. "I'd like you to meet your new assistant manager." I step out from behind Derek and give the girls jazz hands. Ta da!

"Omigod Jane! That is so cool!" Sarah squeals.

"Totally!" Em agrees. I'm so glad she's not mad that I went and talked to Derek right after she turned down the job.

"Yeah, yeah, somebody's got to do it," Derek interjects.

"Your faith in me is underwhelming, Derek," I say, and pat

him on the back. He shoots me daggers with his eyes before heading to his office. Okay, the pat might have been a bit much. Just because we are both management now doesn't mean we should touch. As soon as Derek is out of earshot we all laugh.

"Seriously, that's great, Jane. I'm glad you took the job," Em says as she hugs me.

Did I mention that she is the greatest best friend ever?

"What are we celebrating?" Gavin, my absolute favorite regular, approaches the counter.

"Hey, Gav! I've just been crowned assistant manager," I tell him.

"That's great!" He reaches over the counter and hugs me, too. I'm getting all the love today. "Congrats!"

"Hey, I've got Gavin," I say to Em and Sarah. "The usual, right?" Gavin comes in almost every day and orders the same thing, a medium iced vanilla latte.

He nods, already handing me the $3.89 in cash. I mark the plastic cup, slide it over to Sarah to make, and lean toward Gavin on my elbows.

"So, what's new with you?" I ask.

"Not too much," he says with a slight hesitation. "Well, that isn't totally true. Anne and I broke up yesterday."

"Ooh, I'm sorry. Are you okay?"

"Yeah. Actually I am pretty okay with it. Our relationship had run its course. I'm too young to be tied down anyway, right?" He laughs.

"Sure! That's a good attitude, Gav. I'm glad you aren't letting it bring you down."

"Medium iced vanilla latte," Sarah bellows, no more than three feet away from us.

"That's my call," he says, picking up his drink and popping in the straw. "See you tomorrow." He takes a sip and heads for the door.

"Later." I smile. "Did you hear that?" I ask, stepping over to the girls, who have begun refilling the cookie and coffee cake trays in the glass showcase.

"Yeah, it's too bad," Em says. "He's a good guy."

"He is," I agree, and wipe down the pick-up counter with a wet white rag. "We should totally set him up with someone." I mentally list all the cool girls that I know.

❧

Small Decaf Soy Sugar-free Hazelnut Caffe Latte

Yuppie, her-hubby-is-off-running-an-empire-while-she-is-teaching-the-baby-Latin-with-low-fat-wheat-alphabet-pretzels, yoga-doing-superwoman, stay-at-home-mommy drink. She's fit, in style, and toting a three-hundred-dollar designer diaper bag on her shoulder and a lackadaisical four-month-old in a BabyBjörn on her front. She's über-smart, probably has a master's in something but has given up her high-profile career to focus on the chosen one, who is already showing superior dexterity with the way he is grasping his Baby Einstein flash cards.

"That will be two ninety-five," Sarah tells the customer as she marks the order on the paper cup and slides it my way. "Think you can stop writing in your notebook long enough to make this drink?"

"Already on it," I say, and toss the notebook under the counter once again. I pour a shot of decaf espresso into the plastic cup, add three pumps of sugar-free hazelnut syrup, and begin foaming the soy milk to pour on top.

"Small decaf soy sugar-free hazelnut caffe latte," I call out as I hand the woman her drink and make the expected cooing noises to the baby.

"So, are you ever really going to tell me what's in the notebook?" Sarah asks.

"It's work-related," I respond. "It's part of my assistant-manager duties. Derek just didn't want me to talk about it before." Okay, I'm totally lying now, but Sarah doesn't have to know that. How do I explain to her what I am doing? I don't think I can. About three months ago I was really bored at work and started doodling in my notebook. This woman came in and ordered a large caramel frappycap and it just sort of hit me that she SEEMED like the large-caramel-frappycap type. Not so current with fashion, kinda frumpy, no clue where the gym is, doesn't mind the five hundred calories in the drink. Like, I could see her somewhere else, outside of Wired Joe's, and know that was her drink. It's a "you are what you drink" philosophy. So I've been documenting people's

18

drinks—all kinds of people. Young and old, skinny and fat, blue-collar and white-collar. It's become my little project.

"Ohhhhhh!" Sarah says, and I can see a look of respect come over her face. God, I am so bad. I glance at Em and she has a "you are so full of crap" look on her face. The glass door opens and we are blasted with the cold air again.

"Hey," I tell Sarah and Em, "I'll be right back. I have to grab a sweater." I race to the break room and grab my faux-fur-trimmed hoodie vest. Doesn't exactly go with the Wired Joe's ensemb', but I'm freezing. I walk back up to the front and see Sarah engaged in conversation with a short (maybe five-three?) slim brunette in her early twenties. She's pretty cute. Smart and simple. Nice style—no thong peeking out of her pants or other fashion disasters. Maybe a medium cappuccino? I race back up to the espresso machine and ask Sarah, "Can I get a drink started?"

"Yeah, this is my friend Simone. She wants a medium dry cappuccino."

Ooh, I was close! She just wants an extra foamy cup. I start to foam the milk for the drink. Friend, huh? Hmm . . . what goes well with a medium dry cappuccino? Maybe a medium iced vanilla latte? I smile, and a plan forms in my mind.

❧

"Hey, girls!" Two of my good friends from elementary school, Ava and Katie, walk into Wired Joe's. Now they both go to St. Pat's, a private high school. "Quitting time," I yell to Em, who is already gathering her things. Ava is really into drama and is the lead in the community theater's rendition of *Mame.* Not only is she drop-dead gorgeous, she can sing circles around anyone I know. Katie wants to be an astronaut one day and already plans on doing an internship at NASA next summer. She is way, way smart.

"No rush," Ava says. "Can I get a quick green tea?"

"Sure." I fill a cup with hot water and drop in a tea bag. "You want anything, Katie?"

Katie shakes her head. "Nah, I'm good. I was actually just hoping to catch a glimpse of the frat boys you keep talking about, Jane."

Ah, the frat boys, Will, Grant, and Adam—total hotties. They are the nineteen-year-old Greek gods that attend the University of Illinois at Chicago and stop in almost every night after class for a drink.

Em smiles. "You mean Jane's groupies? They didn't come in tonight. Maybe they have dates?"

"They so do not!" I say. "Well, at least I hope Will doesn't. He's the future Mr. Turner." All the girls erupt in laughter.

"So, why are they Jane's groupies?" Ava asks.

"Because they want only Jane to make their drinks," Em answers. "I think she slips in something extra, if you know what I mean."

"Oh, shut up!" I laugh. "I don't even want to know what you are implying. Besides, what can I slip into espressos over ice?" Adam and Grant always order a three-shot espresso over ice and Will always orders a five-shot espresso over ice. God, he is so cool. I slip on my slim brown-suede jacket, grab my notebook, and sling my one-week's-pay-costing coffee-colored handbag over my shoulder.

"I don't know," Em says, "but there has to be a reason they always want you to serve them."

"Couldn't it just be that I'm gorgeous?" I suggest with the most serious face I can muster.

"Oh . . . sure," Em says. "Your uniform is a huge turn-on." Everyone giggles again.

"All right, all right, are you three ready to go?" I ask.

"Yeah, let's get moving," Katie adds, and we head out the door into the dark to pile into her tiny red Ford Focus illegally parked on the side of the road. "Are we going right to Jen's party?" She starts the car and pulls out onto Wabash. Jen is Katie's college friend who goes to Columbia College. Jen's parents rented an apartment for her so that she wouldn't have to slum it in the dorms.

"No. Can we stop at Em's apartment first so we can change?" I ask. Like I want to hit a party in my white turtleneck and black pants.

"No problem," Katie says, and heads the six blocks to Em's place. When we get there Em and I jump out of the car and promise to be back shortly. We race up the two flights of stairs to her apartment and head for her bedroom. Thankfully, Em's mom is out tonight and won't get to voice an opinion on our clothing choices. I immediately start rummaging through Em's closet looking for something cute to wear. As a bonus to being best friends, we both are almost the same height (I'm five-six and she's five-seven), and we both wear the same size. We are constantly raiding each other's closets.

I finger a pink fake cashmere sweater with my left hand and flip open my cell and dial with my right. My mom will kill me if I don't call to check in.

"Hello?"

"Hey, Mom."

"Hi, sweetie . . . on your way home?" Mom says.

"Not exactly. I'm at Em's." I pull a silver scoop-neck sweater out of the closet, hold it against myself, and turn to show Em. She shakes her head no.

"How was your day?" Mom asks, and I can hear tapping in the background. She's obviously typing on the computer while talking to me.

"Great, actually. Derek made me assistant manager."

"Oh, honey, that's fantastic! It won't interfere with school though, will it?"

I doubt it. "No, of course not. Hey, Mom, is it okay if Em, Katie, Ava, and I go hang out at Jen's?" Not a lie. We will be hanging out at Jen's. Along with fifty of her closest friends.

"Okay, Jane, but be home before midnight."

" 'Kay."

"And keep your phone on."

"Uh-huh."

"Love you," Mom says.

"Love you, too. Bye."

"All cool?" Em asks when I hang up.

"Yep." I return my attention to Em's closet.

"Hey, that was funny what you were telling Sarah about your notebook tonight." Em eyes the notebook that I threw on her bed as she slips on her new skinny jeans and lies back on her bed to button them.

I laugh. "That girl is so nosy. I was getting sick of her asking me about it." I pick up a pair of Em's black leggings and a white-and-black striped skirt and hold them against myself while looking in her mirror.

"So, Dr. Freud, how long is your study of people's coffee habits going to go on?" Em has read through some of my descriptions before and thinks they are hilarious. And accurate, of course.

"I don't know. It's fun and pretty fascinating. I can tell so much about people from their drinks. I actually got an idea tonight that I'm thinking about trying out," I say.

"Yeah? What's that?"

"Well, it really depends on how willing my *subjects* are."

"Oh god, just tell me I'm not one of your 'subjects,'" she pleads, stopping to look at me before she continues to outline her right eye with dark brown pencil.

"Boring ol' medium-hot-chocolate you?" I say. "Nah. Besides, you have a man already." Em has been dating the ever reliable Jason Jones since freshman year in high school. I swear they are going to get married one day.

"Well, I don't see him around tonight, do you?" she says. "And sometimes I get a coffee hot chocolate, so there."

"You told me."

"But seriously, do tell. What does having a man have to do with this?"

"Well," I start, not sure how exactly to say it. "You know how earlier tonight I was telling you how awesome Gavin is and how we should set him up with someone?"

"Yeah . . ." she says, sitting down next to me on the bed.

I flip open my book to "medium iced vanilla latte." "Look." Em quickly reads my entry.

Medium Iced Vanilla Latte

Smart, sweet, and gentle. Sometimes soft-spoken but not a doormat. Loyal and trustworthy. A good friend. Decent looks and body.

"What about it?" Em asks.

"Hold on." I flip through the pages of my notebook again. "Now read this."

Medium Dry Cappuccino

Smart and simple. Fit and fairly good-looking. A little timid and soft-spoken but probably a powerhouse if ever tested. A good friend.

"Okay . . . where is this leading?" Em is totally confused now.

"Don't you see? They're perfect for each other!" I squeal.

"The drinks? What are you going to do with them?"

"Not the drinks," I say, exasperated, "the people. The people who drink these drinks are PERFECT for each other."

"Really? You think so?"

I nod. "And I'm going to prove it. I'm going to hook them up."

"Who?" Em asks.

I sigh and roll my eyes. "Gavin and Simone!"

"Simone?"

"Yeah, Sarah's friend," I say.

"Ohhhhhh . . ." A smile spreads across Em's face. "I can kind of see that! A little coffee matchmaking, eh?"

"A little *Espressology*," I answer, smiling back.

❧

We arrive at Jen's apartment and knock on the door. No one hears us because the music is turned up and we just walk in. The place is packed, mostly with Columbia kids whom I don't know. Katie and Ava disappear almost immediately into the crowd and leave Em and me standing there. Someone slips a cold bottle of beer into my hand. Yuck. Beer is gross. I look up.

"Thanks," I say to the cute blond boy smiling at me. He looks familiar.

"No problem. Jane, right?" he asks.

"Yeah," I reply. "Do I know you?"

"Cam. Cameron White. I sit behind you in English. Of course, I haven't seen you in a couple of weeks." Oh . . . now I remember this guy. He's in my English class at the college.

"Yeah," I say. "How's class going?"

"I can't complain. It's pretty easy really. We only have the four papers to write this semester. Are you coming back to class?"

"Oh yeah . . . for sure. Just been busy. Well, there's my friend. I'll talk to you later." I zigzag through the crowd away from him, setting my unopened bottle of beer down on an end table, and run smack into Simone.

"Hi," I tell her. "I was just talking about you a little while ago. That's so crazy to run into you here." She looks at me like I'm a psycho. "Do you remember me?" I ask. "I met you earlier tonight . . . at Wired Joe's?" She's still looking at me like I'm going to drag her out to an alley and turn her into soup. I pull my long dark-brown hair away from my face and twist it up on my head. "Now picture me with a blue apron on and a foaming pitcher in my hand." A look of recognition comes over her face and she smiles.

"Oh yeah, you made my coffee earlier. It was good. Thanks."

"Sure. Glad you liked it. Hey, listen, are you single?" She looks at me funny again. "Not for me, of course!" I quickly add. "I just know the PERFECT guy for you." She relaxes.

"Oh, well, I generally don't do the blind date thing . . ." she starts.

"You wouldn't really have to. Just let me introduce you. Come into Wired Joe's the next time I work." I quickly go over my schedule in my mind. "Monday afternoon around sixish. His name is Gavin and he's so awesome; he comes in and gets a drink about that time every day. You can get a look at him first and decide if you want to meet him. Then I can just casually introduce you. I swear you guys are PERFECT for each other," I repeat.

"Okay. Why not? I can at least come in and get a drink, right?" she says.

"Cool!" I'm jazzed that my first Espressology test is about to take place. "I'll see you then." I smile and head off to find Em.

3

My classes are so, so hard." Em sets her elbows on the small wooden table and rubs her eyes with the back of her hands. We're sitting at a table next to the bathroom at Wired Joe's, waiting for our shift to start. There is an inch-long string sticking off the seam of Em's black fake-leather shoe and it is driving me crazy. I must get her away from SuperMart shoes and into a decent shoe store. "I was up until three a.m. working on a paper for my lit class."

"I know what you mean. I'm tired, too," I say with a yawn, stretching my arms over my head. Though I'm not tired from school, but rather from catching up on last week's TiVo'd *All My Children* episodes last night.

"How are your classes going?" Em asks. How are they going? Good question.

"I just got off the phone with my mom and she asked the same thing," I say, attempting to avert the question.

"And what did you say?" she persists.

Well, shoot. That didn't work. "Um . . . okay. I guess."

"What's wrong? Is that chemistry class at the college getting you down? I heard that it's hard."

"No . . . not really." It can't get me down if I'm not there, right? Em looks up at me quizzically and props her head on her right fist.

"Why haven't you been talking about school lately?" She studies my face. I hate when she does this.

"It just isn't that exciting," I lie, trying to look innocent. Em's eyes narrow and she rubs her chin with her index finger. "You're the one with all the interesting classes. You know how boring my schedule is," I add. My classes are on the other side of the school from Em's, so even when I do go I rarely see her.

"Really? Just nothing exciting to talk about? What are you studying in your classes?" She continues to look at me. Uh-oh. Her stares are relentless—I'm doomed.

"What?" I ask, shifting uncomfortably in my chair for a few seconds. "Oh fine, fine! I haven't gone to classes in a couple of weeks. Happy?"

"Jane!" she says, exaggerating the "a." "Why haven't you been going to classes?"

"Because," I whine, "they're boring! When will I ever need

to know how to make a cheese soufflé? And I suck in ceramics. Even my grandma wouldn't want one of my spun pots. Seriously. None of this stuff will matter when I'm designing red-carpet gowns in fashion school."

"You can't skip classes, though. You'll get kicked out of school."

"I haven't gotten in trouble yet."

"*Yet* is the key word here," Em says, and frowns. "And what about your college credit courses?"

"I don't like the college either."

"Why not?" she asks.

"It's . . . not what I expected. I want to go to school to study fashion, not stupid English and chemistry. And the people are weird. It's all like, people who couldn't make it into real colleges and old people returning to school. I just don't like it," I say, pouting now.

"So what are you going to do? Just not go? You have to go."

"Why?"

Em sighs and I feel a lecture looming. "Jane, I know you think senior year is just a blow-off year, but it isn't. What if the School of the Art Institute asks to see your grades from this year? What are you going to do then?"

"They wouldn't do that. Would they?"

"They might. Do you really want to take the chance?" she asks. Hmph. We're both silent for a moment. "Just try. Will you go to classes tomorrow?"

"Fine, whatever. Can we talk about something else now?"

"Only if you promise to go to school tomorrow," she retorts.

"Omigod, Mom, I promise, I promise! Jesus!" I say, annoyed.

"Okay, fine, I'll drop it then." She looks victorious. "How much time do we have left?"

"About five minutes," I answer, alternately tapping my left index and middle fingers on the table. "Ooh, did I tell you what is going down tonight?" I suddenly cheer up.

"No, what?"

"Sarah's friend Simone is coming in. I'm going to introduce her to Gavin. He doesn't know it, though, so I'm crossing my fingers that it goes well."

"I hope it does." A slow smile spreads across her face. She's looking at the door.

"What?" I ask, and turn around to see what or whom she is looking at. My frat boys are walking into the store, with Will in the lead.

"Hey, guys!" I call. "You're early today. Gimme a minute and I'll come help you." I race into the break room and throw down my purse and coat, tie on my apron, and get back up front in fifteen seconds flat. Daisy, my thirtysomething too-tight-clothes-wearing floozy co-worker is flirting with my boys, and I want to take a rolled-up paper and smack her in the nose. Heel, Daisy! Heel! "I got it, Dais. Take a break," I tell her. Her mouth opens in protest and I give her my best raised-eyebrow, "I'm the assistant manager, do what I say" look and it actually works! Power is so cool. Daisy doesn't say a word and slips away. "Okay, guys, the usual?" I take my place behind the register.

"Absolutely," Will replies with a killer smile. Man, he is hot. All three of the guys are good-looking, but he is just amazing. He's wearing a dark blue button-down shirt open at the neck, jeans faded so perfectly they could only be bought that way, and dark brown sneakers. His broad chest and shoulders make his loose-fitting brown corduroy jacket hang perfectly on him.

"So, you guys on your way to a fraternity meeting?" I ask in my flirty voice. At least I hope it sounds flirty.

"Not tonight," he answers, flashing his perfectly straight white teeth. "We're actually on our way to an engagement party for one of the senior brothers at a restaurant a few blocks down."

"That sounds fun!" I say. I make the shots of espresso and pour them into each waiting cup.

"Eh." He shrugs and bats his big beautiful midnight-blue eyes at me. "It'd be more fun if you were there." What? Be still my beating-out-of-my-chest heart, did he just ask me out? Or is he just being cute and funny?

"Oh . . . um . . . well . . ." I stammer. Cute boy flirts and I turn into a moron. I must regain a grip on the situation. They don't know I'm not as cool as I seem. Think, Jane, think. Must respond with something clever. "You'll have to try to get along without me—I'm making espressos all night," I return. That sounded okay, didn't it? Not great, but not totally lame. I hear a giggle from back by the display of fifteen-dollar seasonal stuffed bears. Em's laughing at me sounding like a dork. Mental note: must kill her later. The other guys are smiling at me now, too. It's hard to think in the face of such cuteness!

"Maybe some other time?" Will suggests, taking his drink and handing Grant and Adam theirs.

"Sure," I say with a smile, and watch them walk out the door and disappear on the busy sidewalk.

Shoot, I forgot to charge them again.

❧

"Why do you keep checking your watch?" Em asks as we walk around the store wiping down the tables. It's strangely slow for six at night.

"I'm waiting for Simone to show up. I hope she doesn't chicken out. She said she'd come in tonight around six so I can casually introduce her to Gavin."

"I think you better come up with Plan B. Here comes Gavin," she says. I turn toward the door to see Gavin walking in. He looks more attractive than usual today in beat-up jeans and a rust-orange sweater over a T-shirt. His loose dark blond curls frame his face perfectly. It's a little too "surfer dude" for Chicago, but it somehow works on him.

"Hi, Gavin!" I say brightly. "I was hoping you'd come in today."

"You were?" He returns my smile.

"Yeah," I answer. "Can you stay for a few? I want to talk to you."

"Sure, you want to sit?"

"Yeah, gimme a second and I'll bring your drink to you."

Gavin walks over to a table at the far end of the store and sits down.

I start to make his iced vanilla latte and Em comes up next to me. "What are you going to talk to him about?"

"No clue. I've got to stall him, though, and see if Simone comes in," I tell her. "Gav," I say, raising my voice. "It's going to be just a minute. I have to run in back for more vanilla." That should buy me some time.

"Okay, I'll be here," he says.

I walk to the storeroom to pretend to look for the syrup and run smack into Derek. "Hey, Derek. How are you doing?"

"Fine," he replies, clearly irritated. "Listen, I just stopped in for a minute; I have a date. You need to do inventory tonight and have the order for next week's supplies faxed over to corporate before you leave. Here you go." He dumps a stack of papers in my hands. Yikes. "You've seen me do it before, right?"

"Oh sure," I say, "dozens of times." Have I seen him do it? Hmm . . . no idea. Well, it can't be that hard.

"Good, then you'll have no problems," he says, brushing some invisible dirt from the right leg of his jeans.

"No problems at all," I say. "Have a great date." He gives

me a sneer and heads for the door. God, I wonder what poor girl he suckered into going on a date with him?

Okay, I think I've stalled long enough. Time to get back to Gavin. I head to the front of the store with a new bottle of vanilla syrup in my hands. Oh, luck! Simone is here.

"Hi, Simone!" I say loud enough for Gavin to hear. "It's SO good to see you!"

"Hi," she replies hesitantly, once again looking at me like I'm a nut job.

"You want a medium dry cappuccino, right?"

"Yeah." She looks at me in puzzlement. "How did you remember?"

"Steel trap." I tap the side of my forehead. "Hey, Gavin," I call, and turn in his direction. "I'm making your drink now. Sorry it took so long getting the syrup." Simone looks at Gavin and I can see her eyebrows rise in appreciation.

"He IS hot," she whispers to me as she hands me her money for the drink.

"And sweet," I tell her. "Hold on and I'll introduce you." I quickly finish Gavin's drink and yell out, "Medium iced vanilla latte."

"That's me, obviously," he says, smiling as he approaches the counter.

"Corporate rules state I must yell each customer's drink at them before handing it over," I say, and both Simone and Gavin laugh. "Gavin, this is my friend Simone. Simone, this is Gavin." They grin at each other.

"Hi," Gavin says.

"How are you doing?" Simone asks.

"Oh, crap," I say, and they both look at me. "Sorry." I smile weakly. "Now I'm missing medium coffee cups. I have to run and get them. I'll be just a minute." Em looks at the stack of cups clearly sitting behind the counter and smirks.

"I'll help you." She follows me to the storeroom. "No cups, huh?" she says once we get there.

"Yep," I reply, opening a cabinet door and retrieving a package of cups. "And I totally need your help carrying them out there, too."

"I figured!" She laughs. "I'll carry one end and you carry the other." We wait another minute and then head back up front. Both Simone and Gavin are still smiling.

I notice Simone write something on a brown recycled-paper napkin and hand it to Gavin. I add a few more cups to the stack already there and make Simone her drink. "Medium dry . . ." I start to bellow, and Simone laughs.

"Right here," she says, taking her drink and turning to Gavin. "Talk to you soon," she tells him.

"Definitely." He watches her leave.

"What did I miss?" I ask innocently.

"We're going to get together this weekend," he says. "Now, what did you want to talk to me about?" Oh, yeah. I told him I had to talk to him, didn't I? Think fast.

"You know, I just wanted to see how you were doing since

your breakup with Anne, but it looks like you are doing fantastically!"

"Yeah, I'm doing well. Thanks for caring," he says, and smiles warmly at me.

"Sure, see you later," I say. Gavin heads out into the cold night air. I turn to Em, who is now beside me at the counter. "I did what I could; it's up to them now."

Em chuckles and begins wiping down the espresso machine.

4

On Tuesday afternoon, I'm walking briskly down Wabash on my way to work, feeling proud of myself. I went back to school today and actually sat through all my morning high school classes and my two afternoon college classes, taking notes and everything. I even swapped e-mails with this girl Courtney in my chemistry class who said she'd help me get up to speed. The college teachers were all really nice and understanding about me being gone the last couple of weeks to take care of my poor sick grandma. (I had to say something, right?) My study hall teacher never even noticed I was gone; my home ec teacher assigned some make-up raspberry tarts and a cheese strudel to cover my missed assignments; and my ceramics teacher was so laid back all he said was that it was "cool" to see me. I walk into the store and instantly I can see that Derek is pissed.

"What's wrong?" I venture, not really wanting to know, in case it has something to do with me.

"What did I ask you to do last night? What did I specifically stop into the store and ask you to do?"

Uh-oh. The inventory. I totally forgot. "Oh, Derek, I'm so sorry. I forgot."

" 'Oh, Derek, I'm so sorry. I forgot,' " he mocks, in a really silly high voice. I so don't sound like that. "Yeah, well, a hell of a lot of good that does me. I guess we just don't need stock for next week, huh?"

"I'm sorry, I really am. Is there anything I can do?" I ask. *Please don't fire me, please don't fire me,* I chant silently in my head.

"You did quite enough," he angrily huffs. I notice Sarah hovering in front of the cash register with a slightly amused expression, pretending not to listen.

"Well, is there someone I can call? We are only half a day late with the order. I'm sure they can still take it."

"Never mind," he says. "I already took care of it."

"We'll still get our stock in for next week, then?" I ask, wondering why he is freaking out at me.

"Yes, we'll still get our stock in for next week." He slams a box of cups into a cabinet and stomps off to his office.

I look at Sarah with my jaw dropped in a "what was that?" look and she mouths, "Bad date."

"Oh." I giggle and she joins me.

"So, hey," Sarah says, "Simone called me a little while ago on my cell. She said that you set her up with Gavin."

"That I did," I say proudly. "Aren't they freakin' cute together?"

"Totally. Simone is in heaven. She said he already called her and they talked for two hours last night. They have a lunch date for tomorrow."

"That's great." I'm happy that my plan seems to be working.

"I didn't know you were into matchmaking. Maybe you can hook me up with someone? I haven't had a date since Halloween."

"Really? You want me to set you up?"

"Sure, why not? Simone is happy and I want in on it, too. Go for it."

"Okay. Let me think about it for a while and I'll see what I come up with."

"Cool," Sarah says. "Hey, are you okay for a few? I'm going to run to the bathroom."

"Yeah, go ahead." I wait until she's gone and then pull out my notebook. Sarah, Sarah, Sarah. Hmm. She's a little more difficult. Sarah is more of a seasonal girl. That is, she changes her drink with each season or holiday. I flip through the pages and finally settle on pumpkin spice latte, her current drink of choice.

"Ah, there we are," I mumble out loud.

Small Pumpkin Spice Latte
Lots of fun and a bit sassy. Up-to-date with all the latest trends and has a bit of an exotic flair. Wants to have a good time and not

be tied down for long. Cute and playful. Likes a good thing but not too much of a good thing. Not the commitment type. She's the kind of friend who is a lot of fun to hang out with and doesn't make you feel like you owe her anything . . .

"You've GOT to be kidding me," Derek says as he steps around the corner, staring directly at my notebook.

Ah, crap. Man, I'm just batting a thousand today with him.

"What do you think you are doing?" he asks, just as two older women with Tammy Faye Bakker makeup jobs walk in and head straight for the counter. "Sarah? Sarah?" he calls out. I stuff my notebook back under the counter.

"She's in the bathroom," I say.

Sarah comes walking quickly toward us, smoothing down her apron. "Sorry about that." She gives us one of those "you know how it is when you have to go" smiles.

"Sarah, cover Jane. Jane, let's go back in my office and talk."

Ugh. This is so not cool. I give Sarah an "it's no big deal" look and follow Derek to his office. I have to think quickly before we get there. I know he is going to yell at me about my notebook, so I need a logical reason for having it up at the counter.

Derek stomps into his office, points to a seat to indicate that I should sit down, and shuts the door behind me.

"What's up?" I ask, playing stupid.

He sighs, sitting heavily into his chair opposite me. "Jane, you understand that you're the assistant manager now, right?"

"Yeah, of course." Duh, Derek, I was totally here last week when you gave me the job.

"Well, then, that means you have to start acting like one. You need to be setting an example for the other employees. You need to be backing me up whenever I need you to do something. First you screw up the inventory, and then I catch you doing your homework while you are working. You've had the job for what, four days now? Maybe I made a mistake in promoting you. Maybe it is too much for you to handle . . ."

"No!" I protest loudly, interrupting his tirade. "I'm totally perfect for this job. And I wasn't doing my homework." Please, I've been back at school for all of eight hours. I haven't reached the point of doing homework yet.

"You weren't?" His eyebrows shoot up and he tightens his lips.

"No. I was working. I was . . ." Hmm . . . what was I doing? "I was coming up with new specialty drinks. I thought maybe we could do an 'Assistant Manager's Specialty Drink of the Week' and feature what I come up with. I was being inventive. Creative. I was being a go-getter. I was 'thinking outside the box.' " Ooh . . . that's a good one.

"Hmm." He seems to consider this. *Believe me, believe me, believe me,* I beam at him with my eyes. "Well, that's not a *bad* idea," he says. I relax into my seat. "But it would have to be a 'Manager's Specialty Drink of the Week.' " He straightens up and gets a little attitude in his voice. "I mean, I think people would want to know what the manager suggests since I AM the highest-ranking person here."

I nod. "Of course."

"And it might raise sales," Derek says. He glances off to the side of his desk where his computer monitor sits and runs his index finger horizontally across his chin. Yeah, I'm sure he's thinking more sales than Todd Stone. "Your idea isn't half bad."

"Thank you!" I beam. Wow, three pats on the back for me for flipping this situation around so quickly.

"So, what did you come up with?" he asks.

Oh, crap.

"Well . . ." I stall for time. "I don't have my notebook with me, but . . ."

"Yes?" he prods.

"What about a soy raspberry mocha with a swirl of caramel?" I suggest, crossing my fingers behind my chair.

"That's gross," he says flatly.

Ah, well, they can't all be winners.

"I'm still working on it," I tell him. "Give me some time."

"You lost me at caramel. But it wasn't a bad try. How about this? Come up with a month's worth of specialty drinks and get back to me with them. Your idea is okay." He gives me an approving nod. Derek actually looks almost happy.

"Thanks, Derek!" I say, and head out of his office.

"Did he demote you?" Sarah asks when I join her in the front.

"Not at all," I respond. "We were just talking about some ways to increase profits."

"Wow," Sarah says, looking impressed.

"Yeah, there really is a lot that comes with being assistant manager," I say in my hoity-toity voice.

"Sounds like it," she replies as she straightens up the straws and picks up wrappers off the counter. "By the way, your friends were just in here."

"Which friends?" I ask.

"Two girls," Sarah answers. "Both thin and blond, but the taller one was really beautiful. I couldn't really tell if she was being sincere or snarky, though. They ordered small nonfat lattes."

"Ugh . . . say no more!" I immediately know whom she is talking about. "They aren't my friends. Not even close. I'm glad I missed them."

"Really?" Sarah questions. "They asked about you."

"What did they say?" I'm not sure I really want to know.

"Well, the taller one specifically said, 'What? My friend Jane isn't here today? Oh shoot, she makes the BEST drinks.' "

"Yeah," I conclude, "she was being snarky."

"Who were they?"

"Just some stupid girls from school last year. They were seniors when I was a junior and not exactly nice to me."

"Oh, how lame are they? I guess they haven't matured at all since high school."

"Nope," I declare, starting to make two small vanilla crème frappycaps a couple of preteens just ordered.

"So, what kind of mood is Derek in now?" Sarah asks.

"Almost decent," I tell her. "I would talk to him now if you need anything."

"I actually do," she says. "I'm hoping he'll let me have the day after Thanksgiving off. I want to hit the Black Friday sales."

"Sounds like fun! But that is one of our busiest days. Everybody wants coffee while they shop. He might not go for it. I would definitely ask him now before he gets on his next tirade." I am so jealous. I'd love to go to the Black Friday sales, but I know for sure he'll have me work that day.

"Okay, be right back," she says, and heads toward Derek's office.

The front door swings open and five police officers walk in. They aren't in the standard-issue police uniform, though. They are wearing faded blue jeans, dark sweatshirts, and black bulletproof jackets with the word POLICE embroidered across the back in white capital letters. I recognize Officer Jake right away. He's been in here a couple of times before and he is definitely hard to miss. In his early twenties, and built like a baseball player, Officer Jake is tall, Italian, and gorgeous. The muscles busting out of his forearms are incredible. You just want to touch them. The other guys with him are decent-looking enough, though maybe a bit older. Officer Jake is definitely the cutie of the group. And single.

"Hey, how's it going?" he bellows out as he approaches the

counter, confidence radiating from him. This guy is definitely comfortable in his own skin.

"Great. What can I get you all?" They each give me their order, but I concentrate on Officer Jake's—a large extra-bold Sumatra with room for cream. Hmm . . . confident, daring, fun, and, well, incredibly hot. He's perfect for Sarah! Now how to get them together?

I make all the officers their drinks and call them out. They take them to one of the bigger tables near the windows. It looks like they are going to sit and talk for a while, so I have a few minutes to devise a hookup plan. I grab a napkin and walk over to the employee bulletin board in the hallway outside the break room.

"Sarah, Sarah, Sarah," I say, scanning the employee call list tacked up on it. Bingo. I scribble Sarah's phone number onto the napkin with a short cute note and hustle back up to the front. Okay, now I have to get it to him. I glance over to the dessert tray in the display case, and a plan forms in my mind. I take out a slice of our signature coffee cake and place it on the napkin, careful not to cover the phone number so it doesn't leave any grease marks and smudge a number. Just then, Sarah returns.

"You were right, Jane. He was in a pretty good mood. He let me take the day off."

"Great. Hey, do me a favor," I say as I start finger-combing Sarah's long black curls and wipe some mascara smudges from under her eyes.

"Um . . . what are you doing?" she asks. "You better not wipe spit on me next."

"I won't. Just take this cake out to that magnificent-looking policeman sitting over by the window." Sarah looks up and sees Officer Jake.

"YUUUUUUMMMMMMMY!" she exclaims, and starts to help me fix her hair. "Here." She holds out her hand and I place the cake in it. I watch Sarah walk up to the table and hand Officer Jake his cake. He grins, looking a little puzzled, but accepts the cake. Sarah tells him something and throws back her head, shaking her curls a bit. She's definitely flirting. She says something else and returns to the counter. I can see that she's hiked up her tight long-sleeve cotton shirt so that a strip of her stomach and back peeks out. She's a pro. He's totally watching her walk away.

Officer Jake and his friends talk for another moment and Sarah and I drool from afar as we watch him take a few bites of the cake. We're drooling over him, of course, though the cake looks pretty good today, too. A call comes over their radios and they all jump up and head for the door. Officer Jake comes by the counter first and waves the napkin at Sarah.

"Thanks for the cake," he says with a wink. "I'll give you a call."

Sarah beams and nods and we both watch him leave. She turns to me, "What the . . . ?"

"There's your hookup."

5

Is it just me, or does this project seem a bit lame to you?" I ask, scooting my chair and desk around so that I can sit face-to-face with Cameron White. Professor Monroe, our English instructor, said our next assignment is a five-to-eight-page biography on someone else in the class. Because of our seating vicinity, Cam and I decided to partner up on this one.

"I don't know," he says with a straight face. "It might be fun to learn about all your deep dark secrets."

I stare at him for a moment, not sure what to say.

"You don't really expect me to tell you my secrets, do you?" I whisper.

"Well, you'll have to give me something good to write about. I want an A." Cam grins at my worried look.

"No way!" I exclaim with a nervous laugh, relieved. "Besides, I'm going first with the questions." I tap my pen on my notebook, purse my lips, and study Cam. He's really not bad-looking at all. He's a little more rugged than the typical guys I see around the city. More like he should be hiking a trail somewhere instead of riding the El train. But he's got really nice blue eyes and he laughs a lot, which makes his face light up.

"You are taking too long to come up with a question. You're kind of scaring me."

"Okay, okay, I'm just trying to come up with some good ones. I think I'm going to start from the present and work my way back, if you don't mind," I say.

"I don't mind. Shoot."

"Okay. Number one, how did you decide to attend Anthony Carter Community College?" I ask.

"That's a good question," Cam says, and I relax a little and prepare to take notes. "I actually got into Indiana University—it's one of the Big Ten schools. They have a decent finance program—that's my major, by the way—and I'd always planned on going there."

"What happened?"

"Well," he says, taking a long pause. "My mom was diagnosed with breast cancer in August."

"Wow," I say, dropping my pen. "I'm really sorry."

"She's doing okay so far," he tells me, "but she's all alone and, well, she needs me right now. The chemo has been rough on her. For the time being, I'm staying home to help her and going to school locally."

"You are, like, the best son ever." I have a sudden respect for Cam. He shrugs.

"My turn. What's your favorite coffee drink?"

"What?" I chuckle. "Are you kidding me? Is this going in my biography?"

"Definitely," he says, with his pen on his paper waiting to write down my answer. "I'm very interested. You already told me you're the assistant manager at the Wired Joe's around the corner, so I'm sure you're an expert on the best drinks."

"That is kind of true." I try to sound modest. "But just because I know a lot about coffee doesn't mean my favorite would be everybody's favorite. It's such an individual thing."

"Still waiting . . ." He feigns impatience.

"Large iced nonfat mocha, no whip," I tell him, and he actually writes it down.

"Hmm . . . interesting." Cam stares at what he just wrote.

"Oh, stop it," I say, shaking my head. I've been analyzing people and their drinks for so long that it's kind of weird having someone analyze me. Just then Professor Monroe interrupts and tells us that class is over for today. I check my watch. Fifteen minutes to get to work.

"I don't have nearly enough here to write a paper on you, so it looks like we're going to have to work on this outside of class. Do you want to meet sometime?"

"Sure," I say, writing my e-mail address down in the upper corner of his notebook. "Gimme your e-mail, too." He writes his in my notebook. "When is this due, anyway?" I ask.

"Next Wednesday. We only have a week, so we'll have to get together soon," he says.

"Let's shoot for Sunday afternoon," I suggest. "I work until four. You can meet me at Wired Joe's and we can work at a table there."

"Cool." He tosses his books in his backpack and walks with me out the classroom door. "See you then."

"See you," I say, buttoning up my tan designer-knockoff jacket (who can afford a real one?) and slipping my backpack over one shoulder. As I head out the door I hear the signal on my phone indicating I have a text message. It says, "J, come over. 911. E."

I type back, "Wrk in 15."

Em responds, "4 real. 911."

"Ok," I type, and slide my phone back into my bag.

∞

I run the three blocks from school to Wired Joe's to let Derek know I'm going to be late for work this afternoon. I tell him I have my period and no tampons so I need to go to the store and he makes an "ew, gross" face. The "just got my period" excuse works on every single male teacher at school—it's good to know it is just as effective in the real world. I leave Wired Joe's and run the six blocks to Em's. I ring her apartment and she buzzes me in. The door is unlocked and I know her mom is at work, so I head in and go straight to her bedroom.

"Must . . . start . . . working . . . out . . . again," I huff and puff, bending over slightly and grabbing my sides. I take a moment to regain my breath and then finally look up at Em. She's lying in a lump on her bed and, oh crap, she's crying.

"What's wrong?" I ask, not entirely sure what to do. I've never seen Em cry before. In the seven years that we've been best friends I've cried plenty and she's always consoled me. Well, until now, that is. I sit down on the bed next to her. "Em, what's wrong?"

Em turns her head from her pillow to look at me. She's a puffy-faced mess. "Jason broke up with me," she whispers.

"What?" I practically scream at her. I can't believe it. Jason and Em have always been so solid. They are the dream couple. "Why on earth would he break up with you?"

Em's face crumples and she drops her head into her pillow again. Her shoulders rise and fall with her crying. I wait for her to stop. She turns her head and looks at me. "He said it isn't working anymore. He said we're too different," she chokes out.

"What does that mean?" I ask.

Em grabs a handful of Kleenex from the box on the desk near her bed. "He thinks I'm too involved with school," she tells me.

"What does he expect? You are taking really hard classes this semester. He should know that you have a lot of work." Em nods her head in agreement. "Not to mention . . . you're going to college next year and then law school. He should get used to all the schoolwork now."

"That's just it," she says. "The prelaw thing. He thinks I'll be too busy with school and study groups to spend any time with him, so we should just end it now."

"Maybe it's not such a bad thing to break up," I say, crossing my arms. "If he can't hack it now while you are in high school, he sure won't be able to when you are in college."

Em's face crumples up again and she buries it in her pillow. Shoot. Wrong thing to say. I knew I was no good at this consoling business.

"Sorry, sorry, sorry," I say. "What can I do to help? Do you want me to try to talk to him?" We all hung out quite a bit last year, so I feel pretty comfortable approaching him about this. We haven't hung out much since the school year started, though. Jason was a year ahead of Em and me and is out of school now. He didn't go to college. He went right to work for his uncle in his construction business and has been pretty busy himself.

"No!" Em screams, sitting straight up. "I didn't tell you the worst part."

Uh-oh. There's more?

"Oh god . . . I'm so embarrassed." She covers her face with her hands.

"It's okay, Em, you know you can tell me anything."

"He's . . . dating someone else. She's . . . a . . . townie," she says.

"A what?" I ask.

"You know, a townie. His uncle lives in a really small suburb of the city. Jason has been spending all his time out there since he started working for him." Em sighs and takes a deep breath. "She's like the town hussy or something. She practically lives at the one little local bar in town. She's twenty-four and she works at the SuperMart full-time."

"Dare to dream," I say.

"It gets worse," Em continues. "He met her bowling." Despite Em's distress. I can't help but grin, putting the whole picture of this girl together. "She's on his league."

"Jason is on a bowling league?!" I practically scream. "What's up with that?" I ask, laughing now. "Do they have team shirts and everything?"

"God, I don't know. And stop laughing—this isn't funny! He's been acting strange ever since he graduated," she says.

"Sounds like it." I mean, seriously, a bowling league? I shudder.

"What am I going to do?" Em whimpers.

"Do you really want my opinion?"

She nods.

"Let him go."

"But we've been together for almost three years!" she protests.

"I know. I'm not saying it will be easy or anything, but he cheated on you, Em. Or I should say he IS cheating on you. And, not that I want to agree with a cheating jerk, but it does sound like you guys are headed in different directions."

Her bottom lip quivers a bit. "I know."

"I'm sorry, Em," I say. "Here, let me call Derek and let him know I can't make it to work after all. I'll tell him I have killer cramps or something. We can hang out tonight."

"Okay. Thanks, Jane," she says, wiping her eyes with the Kleenex.

6

"How are you doing today, Em?" I ask in the break room of Wired Joe's. I just finished my shift, and Em is coming on to work the afternoon-till-close shift. It has been strangely slow for a Sunday.

"I don't know. All right, I guess," she replies in a melancholy voice.

I fold up my blue apron and shove it in my bag as she slips hers on and ties it behind her back.

"I know it doesn't seem like it, but things really will get better," I assure her, looking in the mirror on the wall to adjust the thick plaid tweed headband in my hair and smooth down my white collared shirt. I wish I'd brought a change of clothes for my meeting with Cam today.

"Yeah, I know. You keep saying that. I'm still waiting for it to happen."

"Well, it won't happen immediately," I say, even though I have no experience in this department, since I've never really had a long-term boyfriend. "What's going on? You sounded better on the phone yesterday morning. I knew you should have come out with Katie, Ava, and me last night. Next time I'm going to drag your butt out so you don't have time to sit around and mope."

"I didn't sit around and mope the whole time," she says. "I saw him."

"You saw Jason?" I spin around to look at her. "Oh, my god, Em, why? Please tell me you didn't do the desperate girl thing and beg for him to take you back." Darn it. I should have kept her company last night. I can be such a sucky friend sometimes.

"No . . . no! Of course not. I'm depressed but not stupid," Em says. "I ran out to Chipotle for a burrito last night and he was there. He looked amazing. He was wearing that big super-soft comfy navy blue sweater that I gave him last Christmas. For just the briefest of moments I wanted to rush up to him and throw my arms around him. But then I noticed he was with *her*. I lost my appetite instantly, so I turned around and went home."

"Oh geez, Em, that's rough. Did he see you?"

"No, I don't think so." We're both silent for a moment.

"What did she look like?" I finally ask.

A slight smile spreads across Em's face.

"Totally lame," she admits.

"Tell me, tell me. I want details."

"Well, for starters she was wearing acid-washed stretch jeans."

"No!" I practically scream, covering my mouth with my hand.

"Yeah, I didn't even know they still made those," she says.

"Maybe she bought them on eBay?" I offer. "You can buy all kinds of crap there."

"Maybe," she echoes. "She also had on a pink-and-green tie-dyed shirt, big pink hoop earrings, and, get this, construction boots."

"Oh, for the love of Brenda Walsh, are you kidding me?" I squeal. "He HAS to have lost his mind. That is so nineties I want to puke."

"I know," Em adds with a little laugh. "I bet the construction boots turn Jason on. Not that I want to picture someone else turning him on." She abruptly stops laughing.

"I can understand that," I say. "Last question, and then we won't talk about her anymore. Promise."

"Okay."

"Hair?"

"Bad perm," Em answers.

"I knew it!" I say, clapping my hands together. I pick up my bag and turn toward the door to leave. "Em"—I turn back around to face her—"maybe you *should* think about letting me set you up with someone. I know we were kidding about it in your room the other night, but it might be good for you. You know, just to get back out in the world and all."

"Huh? No." She makes a face.

"Oh, come on," I urge. "Just one date. And only if the coffee beans speak to me."

"I don't know . . ."

"Okay, promise me you'll think about it. I'm going to grab a drink and get out there for my meeting with Cam. Have a good shift. And don't worry. It really will get better."

"I hope so," she says, and follows me to the front of the store.

꿇꿇

Cam is sitting in one of the two big blue velvet comfy chairs in the front corner of the store. The blue-and-white neon sign of the Wired Joe's logo is hanging behind his head and he's listening to something on his iPod. I plop down in the chair opposite him.

"Hey, Cam."

"Hey, Jane." He turns off his iPod and pulls out the earbuds. "How's it going?"

"Really good." I set my iced mocha down on the small table between us. I notice that he already has a drink. "I would have made you something for free," I say.

"That's okay," he says. He picks up his drink and takes a swig.

"What did you get, anyway?" I ask, curious to see what his drink is. I'm having a hard time pegging this one.

"Toffee nut latte," he says.

"Toffee nut latte?" I repeat, almost accusingly. It's been a while since I've come across a toffee nut latte. I close my eyes and try to mentally picture the entry in my notebook.

Toffee Nut Latte

Definitely not what you expect. Very hot . . . very sexy . . .

My eyes spring open and I can feel myself blushing fiercely. Is that what the entry really says? I wonder if I can casually peek into my notebook . . .

"Yeah, what's wrong with that?" he asks.

"Oh, nothing. Nothing at all. I just didn't see it coming," I say, still feeling flush.

"You are kind of weird sometimes, Jane."

"So true," I agree.

We start working on our project, and I find that I'm having a really good time with Cam. He is SO funny. He's telling me all kinds of stories about growing up and the kids he played with on his block. Like this one time, he and his friend Vinnie walked up and down the sidewalks yelling, "Lassie! Come home!" People would stop and ask them what was wrong and they would say that they lost their collie Lassie (as in the TV dog Lassie) and people were actually helping them look. It was all good and funny until Cam's mom went to the school PTO meeting and the president asked her if they'd found their dog. Which, of course, was nonexistent. She was totally embarrassed and Cam got in mega trouble.

Em is at the espresso machines making the drinks while Wendy, one of our older baristas, is working the register. I can see Em occasionally watching us and I give her a smile.

"Who are you smiling at?"

"Oh, that's my best friend, Em," I answer. "She's awesome."

"That is really cool that you guys get to work together."

"Yeah, it totally is," I agree.

The front door of the store opens and I feel a knot forming in my stomach. Melissa walks in, sans sidekick Ginny this time. A look of repulsion must have come over my face because Cam says, "What's wrong?"

"Nothing. I just suddenly don't feel so well."

"Do you need to use the bathroom?" he inquires with concern.

"No." Great. Now he thinks I have diarrhea or something. Melissa saunters right on over to us.

"Jane!" she sings, like she and I are the nearest and dearest. "How are you? I'll have a small nonfat latte."

"I'm not working, Melissa," I say through gritted teeth.

"Oh, you are so cute, Jane. Isn't she so cute?" she asks, turning to Cam. "Okay then, I'll have that latte."

"Seriously . . . not working," I repeat.

"What do you mean you're not working?" Melissa asks. Is she kidding? Usually being confronted with Melissa Stillwell turns me into a meek little kitten, but I'm not feeling so meek today. She's totally embarrassing me in front of Cam.

"Take the literal translation," I say. "I'm not working . . . not making drinks . . . can't help you out. *No estoy trabajando.* Go up to the register and place your order there." Wow, that felt good. Though saying it in Spanish was probably a bit much, and I might get a little sarcasm backlash.

"Oh! I'm sorry," she says. "Are you on a date? Are you one of Jane's relatives?" she asks Cam.

"What?" Cam turns to me with a puzzled look. I feel my face flush red. Oh, my god, I'm going to hurt this girl one of these days. I look down at my notebook and pray for her to just go away.

"Next," Em bellows out, registering the situation. "What do you want, Melissa? I'll take your order." Em to the rescue again. Melissa looks reluctant to go, especially right in the middle of a dig at me. She glances at her watch.

"Well, I do have to hurry. I AM meeting a date soon. No relation," she adds, looking pointedly at me. She walks toward Em, sashaying her hips all the way (which I'm sure is for Cam's benefit), and places her order. If evil glares could do damage, she would be hurting right now.

"What was that all about?" Cam asks with a stunned expression. I take a deep breath and hope that my face is returning to a normal color.

"Just a nasty girl who went to my school last year," I explain.

"She seems like a real witch," he says.

"Oh . . . she definitely is." We both watch Melissa take her drink and then walk back toward the front door.

"Later, Jane!" she calls on her way out, but I don't respond.

"Definitely not a nice girl," Cam says.

"Uh-uh. She made it her mission to torture me junior year. She graduated and I thought that was that, but no, she recently rediscovered me here."

"Why don't you just punch her in the face?" he asks.

"Punch her in the face?" I repeat. "I don't know. That is so boy. Besides, I've never really punched anyone. I don't think I would be very good at it."

His face breaks into a grin. "I'm kidding, Jane."

"Oh." I nod.

"Seriously, have you tried talking to her?"

Talk to Melissa? The words *pointless* and *aggravating* spring to mind. "No," I say. "It's no use. She's like this every time I see her."

"Well," he says, "maybe try to get her one-on-one. You can't just let her keep making fun of you like that."

I sigh and begin to explain to him my problem with girls like her and how I've always turned from confident and assured to a weak doormat in about three seconds flat.

Cam scribbles in his notebook.

"That was off the record. Don't put that in your paper."

"We'll see," he teases.

"You better not," I say, slapping him playfully on the

shoulder. And a muscular shoulder at that. We're both laughing and I'm suddenly struck with a bit of genius. Cam is so much fun. I wonder if he'd be a good match for Em? Maybe not a forever-and-ever love connection, but they'd have a good time for now. Though that whole toffee nut latte thing kind of throws me for a loop. But then again, isn't there a super-yummy European nutty chocolate spread? So a toffee nut latte might go with a coffee hot chocolate. Maybe.

"Earth to Jane."

"Huh?" I say, coming out of my thoughts and looking at him.

"What are you thinking about?" Cam asks. "You just went away there for a moment."

Ah, what the heck. There's no time to check my notebook. I'll just have to go with a gut feeling on this one.

"I was thinking about you and my friend Em. I was thinking maybe you should take her out sometime. You guys would be really cute together." A flicker of something comes over his face. Is that pain? No—what could be painful about taking a cute girl out? Is he hurt? Did I say something wrong?

"You"—he stumbles a bit—"want me to take out your friend?"

"Yeah. Em is awesome. She's so sweet and fun to be around. You'll love her."

Cam looks down at his hands for a moment and bites his bottom lip. He lifts his head back up and meets my eyes.

"Okay. If you want me to, I'll take her out," he says in a monotone voice. Geez, I would think he could muster some enthusiasm. I hope he is more fun on their date.

"Great. I'll set it up."

◈

I give Em's information to Cam. He tosses his notebook into his forest-green backpack and says he'll see me in class. I gather my stuff and head back up to the counter to chat with Em while she makes drinks.

"So," I say, reaching past the service table and grabbing a large straw to play with.

"So, what?" Em echoes, checking the temperature on the pitcher of frothed milk.

"What do you think of the war in the Middle East? Duh, Em, what do you think I mean? What do you think of my friend Cam? I totally saw you checking him out. Don't even try to lie."

"What?" She blushes. "I wasn't checking anybody out."

"Yeah . . . okay . . . whatever," I say. "Do you want to go on a date with that guy you weren't checking out?"

Em slams the frothing pitcher on the table, spilling some, and looks at me with her eyebrows shot up.

"What did you bloody hell do?" she hisses at me, narrowing her eyes.

"Hey, calm down." I grab a handful of napkins and stretch

over the counter to clean up the spilled milk. "Cam is great. It would be a fun thing, casual, just for laughs. Nothing serious at all, I swear."

"No, Jane. I told you I wasn't ready."

"Well, I'm not asking you to pick out china patterns with the guy. Just go on one date," I say.

"I . . . I can't," she says. "I haven't dated anyone besides Jason in years."

"Exactly! That is why Cam is the perfect choice for a first post-Jason date. Seriously, Em, he'll have you laughing all night." I can see Em soften and consider the idea.

"I don't know. I don't know if I'm ready."

"Well, just chat with him online first. I gave him your IM screen name and your e-mail address," I say.

"What?! I never really had a choice in the matter, did I?" she asks.

"Not really, but if a long-term boyfriend ever breaks up with me, I'll expect you to return the favor."

"Well," she says, wiping the sides of the milk pitcher with a wet towel, "he is pretty cute."

I grin. "That he is."

7

On Wednesday, I've only been working for about an hour and Sarah and I are doing a quick cleaning. There was a mom in here when my shift began who let her one-year-old tear the place apart. He was bowling with an apple and the yogurt smoothie containers from the refrigerator case and building a pyramid with pound packages of coffee. She sat there the entire time looking adoringly at him and I was wondering just how big of a mess he was going to leave me to clean before the next rush of customers. I reached my breaking point when he pulled down all of the coffee travel mugs and walked around the store passing them out. As I was about to finally say something to his mom, she swooped him up, blew raspberries into his neck, and left the store, not even giving a backward glance at the wreck her toddler tornado had left.

I am putting the mugs away when I suddenly feel a presence behind me. I glance over my shoulder. It's a slightly pleased Derek. His right hand is poised in midair, but then he quickly pulls it down to his side. I think he was going to pat me on the back.

"Hey," I say. "How's it going, Derek?"

"Good. These are good." He waves a paper in his left hand at me. It's my list of "Manager's Specialty Drinks" for the month of December.

"Thanks."

"Keep it up." He nods at me awkwardly and then walks quickly toward his office. I step behind the counter to wait on the next customer. Sarah joins me.

"Was that Derek . . . being nice?"

"Yeah. Looks weird on him, doesn't it?"

"Totally." She giggles. "Hey, I didn't thank you for setting me up with Officer Scrumptious."

"What happened?" I ask excitedly. "Did he call you? Did you go out?"

"Yes and yes," Sarah answers. "He's so awesome. He called me the next day and we met for drinks. We hit it off right away so afterward we decided to go dancing. He is *such* a good dancer. The way he moves his body. Omigod."

"That good, huh?"

"Mmm-hmm." She has a dreamy look on her face.

"Well, I'm two for two now. First Gavin and Simone, and then you and Officer Jake. I'm setting up my friend Cam with Em now."

"You're becoming the local matchmaker," she says.

"Yeah. I guess I kind of am." Just then the door opens and in walk my frat boys. "Oh my gosh, is it after five already?"

Sarah nods. "Yeah, it's five-twenty."

Ugh. No time to fix my hair or check my makeup. I turn my head and try to subtly sniff my shirt. Did I put on my wildflower body spray this morning? Can't remember. I squirt a tiny bit of vanilla syrup into my palm and dab a bit behind each ear. Yeah, it seems a little gross, and quite frankly sticky, but it is here and fast, and, well, now I smell delicious. I quickly pinch my cheeks to give them some color. I don't actually think it will make me look any better, but my grandma always told me, "Give your cheeks a little pinch whenever you are about to talk to a cute boy." And Will is as cute as they come, so I pinch away.

"Are you okay?" Will asks, and I quickly take my hands away from my face.

What, did he fly across the store to the counter? "Sure!" I say, grinning ear to ear. "How are you doing today?"

He frowns slightly. "I could be a lot better. I overslept and missed my math class. Then I failed my history quiz. Not good."

"I'm so sorry," I say. "At least Thanksgiving is tomorrow and you'll get a break."

Will nods. "That's true. What about you? Any special plans for tomorrow, Jane?"

"Just the normal family thing," I say. "My mom always hosts Thanksgiving."

"That's sweet," he says with a warm tone in his voice. "We're not really doing the whole Thanksgiving thing."

"Why not?"

"We all"—he points to himself and his friends—"got roped into some fraternity duties this weekend and can't go home. We're going to get together with a group of friends and just watch football games and order pizzas."

"That sounds like fun!" I say. And I seriously mean it. I would so rather be sitting at Will's frat house eating pizza tomorrow instead of sitting next to my sloppy uncle Ed, who somehow manages to spill gravy on my shirt at every holiday meal.

"You're more than welcome to join us," Will offers.

"Seriously?" I ask a little too eagerly.

"Yeah," he says, and laughs.

Now I look like an idiot again. I really need to calm down. But this is almost a date!

"Well, here," I say, shoving a piece of paper and pen at him, "write down your info and I'll call you if I can get out of my family thing."

Will jots down a phone number and passes the paper to me. I fold it up and slip it into my pocket.

The boys take their drinks and head for the door. Will pauses and turns back around. "Maybe we'll see you tomorrow."

"Maybe," I say.

"Niiiiice," Sarah says.

"I know, right?"

⊱⸺⊰

Thanksgiving Day starts out just as I expected. Dad, Uncle Ed, Grandpa Turner, and my cousins Nathan (whom I still haven't forgiven for the whole homecoming debacle last year) and Kevin are all parked on the couch in front of the TV watching football. Mom, Grandma Torreni, Aunt Sally, and my super people-pleasing cousin Susie are all cooking a ton of food in the kitchen. I don't know where to go. I don't want to cook and I hate football. I consider sneaking back into my room to read the new book I bought last week when I hear my name.

"Jaaaaaaaane," my mom calls.

Oh crap. I head toward the kitchen. The silver fixtures and appliances gleam and the pumpkin-colored walls give the room a warm feeling. I stand outside the door, hoping that is as close as I will have to get.

"There you are," Mom says. "Come here and hold the turkey's legs apart so I can pull out the guts." Mom is standing next to the sink holding on to the pimply-skinned legs of a gigantic turkey.

"What?" I twist my face in disgust. "No way, that is so gross."

"Jane, I need you," Mom says in a stern voice now.

"Um, I'd really rather not."

"I can help you, Auntie Cheryl," Susie says, and I roll my eyes.

"No, Susie, you are elbow-deep in stuffing. Jane, NOW," Mom orders.

I'm not going to get out of this.

"Oh, for god's sake," I mutter under my breath as I join my mom at the sink. "Fine, I'm here. What do I have to do?"

"Grab each leg with one of your hands and spread."

"You are going to at least give me gloves to wear, right?" I ask.

"It's just a turkey, Jane. Now grab."

I tentatively grab each of the turkey's legs in my hands and I swear I'm about to retch. The turkey totally looks like a big fat baby with its peachy wet skin. Its wings are both folded in close to its chest and I really think I am going to lose it right here on the spot. I turn my head and close my eyes.

"Okay, now spread," Mom says. I yank the turkey's legs apart and I feel a little dizzy. I don't know why, but I turn back to the sink and open one eye to see what Mom is doing. Just then I see her whole forearm disappear into the turkey and then reappear with a mound of gushy red turkey innards.

"Oh, my god!" I yell. I let go of the turkey legs, cover my mouth, and run out of the kitchen to the bathroom.

I hear my mom sigh and Susie say, "Don't worry, Auntie Cheryl, I've got it."

But I don't even care. Let Susie hold the turkey's legs. I'm so not going back in there.

After a moment of dry heaving over the toilet, I step to the sink and squirt three large globs of antibacterial soap onto my hands. I scrub for a few moments, trying to erase any evidence of the last few minutes.

I head to my room to think about what to do next. Well, I'm certainly not about to eat turkey after what I've just seen. A smile spreads over my face as I remember Will's invitation yesterday and I decide to attempt slipping out and hitting his Thanksgiving celebration. I pick up yesterday's pants off the top of my laundry pile and search for Will's phone number. I find the piece of paper, grab my cell phone off my desk, and climb up on my bed to make the call. I dial his number, mentally preparing what I'm going to say as I hear someone pick up.

"I'm sorry, the wireless number you are trying to reach is not in service," a mechanical woman's voice says to me.

"What?" I say. I take the phone away from my ear and look at it. "That can't be right." I hit END on my cell phone and then dial the number again. The same robot chick answers.

"I'm sorry, the wireless number you are trying to reach is not in service."

I snap my phone shut and lean back on my pillows. I wonder what happened. Did his parents find out he failed his quiz and turn off his cell phone service? No, that would be overly dramatic, wouldn't it?

I hope he is okay. What if he got in a terrible accident? He could have been standing too close to the train tracks on his way home last night when he heard someone yell his name. Only it wasn't him they were calling: it was a girl named Jill. But it was too late; he turned too fast, lost his footing, and fell right onto the tracks. Before he could scramble off, WHOOSH! He was run over by the orange line! Oh, no. Poor Will. He's probably lying in a hospital bed somewhere calling out my name.

"Jane . . . Jane . . . Jane . . ."

But no. That doesn't make sense either. His phone would have just forwarded to voice mail if it had been squashed by a train. That, and I'm sure there probably would have been something on the news.

I lie on my bed for a few more minutes and then I sit bolt upright, suddenly feeling a little nauseated again. Did he give me a fake phone number? No. I mean, he wouldn't do that, right?

I try to read my book, which is really pretty good, but it doesn't take my mind off the whole Will phone number thing. I decide to go on instant messenger and see if there is anyone else online to talk to. I log on and a moment later see my buddy list window appear. I scan the list—Megan87, Beerfreak111, HotButterKisses, and EM2009. Yes! Em is online. I quickly send her a message.

baristachick09: EM!! OMG, I'm so glad u r online!!!

EM2009: Hey, Happy Turkey Day!

baristachick09: Seriously, no turkey talk. : (

EM2009: Y? What's wrong?

baristachick09: Em, am I totally lame? Do u think Will likes me?

EM2009: Will, who gave you his #, Will? Totally.

baristachick09: That's just it.

EM2009: ???

baristachick09: I called the #. Not in service.

baristachick09: r u still there?

EM2009: Yeah. Just thinking.

baristachick09: It's bad, right?

EM2009: I dunno. Maybe, maybe not. Maybe something happened?

baristachick09: Like what?

EM2009: I don't know, ask him when u c him.

baristachick09: Maybe. : (

EM2009: Cheer up. It's a holiday! :)

baristachick09: Y r u in such a good mood?

EM2009: :) :) :)

baristachick09: What? Tell me.

EM2009: Cam=AWESOME.

baristachick09: u talked to him?

EM2009: Yeah. A few times. We were just IMing but he had to go help cook. OMG, what a sweetie.

baristachick09: He is.

EM2009: We r going out tomorrow night.

baristachick09: u r? Cool.

EM2009: u r ok with that, right? r u mad?

baristachick09: No.

EM2009: r u sure?

baristachick09: Yeah.

EM2009: Remember—u set us up . . .

baristachick09: I know, I know. Not mad, promise. Just thinking about the Will thing.

EM2009: Don't let it ruin your day. 4real.

baristachick09: Ok.

EM2009: My mom is calling. Got2go. c u tomorrow, k?

baristachick09: c u.

I log off and sit back in my desk chair. I know I set Cam and Em up and I am happy that Em is happy but . . . I don't know. I guess I'm a little surprised that they've hit it off so quickly. They're both awesome, so I guess I shouldn't be too surprised. Ugh. It's probably this whole Will thing making me feel weird. I push away from my computer, climb back into bed, and throw my fuzzy pink covers over my head. Maybe a nap will help.

❧

It's still dark out after I've slowly trudged into the store. I can't believe I have to work this early, but it's Black Friday, our busiest day of the year. Everyone comes in for coffee to keep warm and awake while they wait in line at electronics or toy stores or wherever else all the big sales are. I'm trying to mentally prepare for the day of craziness when I see a sleepy-eyed Em come in.

"Hey, Jane," she says. She yawns and walks to the break room to put her stuff away. She comes back up front and helps me arrange the chairs.

"Tired?"

She yawns. "Uh-huh."

"I'll go make some drinks to wake us up."

"Good idea."

"Have you tried the maple macchiato yet?" I ask.

"No, but I'll drink anything this morning. I need something to kick me into gear."

I step behind the counter and turn on the espresso machine. Derek comes out from his office and gives me a look.

"Jane, I need to see you," he says.

Shoot. He looks pissed. What could I have done now? I follow him back to his office and take a seat.

"What's up?" I ask.

"Well," he starts, "I don't want to take the word of one employee over another, but if there is something going on I need to stop it right now." I stare at him blankly.

"What are you talking about?"

"You've been doing well lately, Jane. Really."

"Okay . . ."

He sighs heavily. "Are you giving out free drinks to your friends?" he asks.

"What?" I hope I sound shocked. "No, of course not! Who would say that about me?"

"I really shouldn't say," he answers slowly, but instantly I know. It's that stupid middle-aged Botox-faced Daisy.

"Daisy told you that, didn't she?" I ask. Derek holds up both hands in protest.

"I really shouldn't say," he repeats, shaking his head from side to side.

"You don't have to," I say. "I know it is her—she is totally jealous of me. And how can you trust someone whose face doesn't move when she talks? You wouldn't even know if she's lying."

Derek smirks at this, but then quickly goes back to stone-faced.

"Okay, like I said, I don't want to take one employee's word over another's. But if you are giving away free drinks, you need to stop immediately. It is grounds for dismissal."

"I'm totally not, Derek," I lie, but mentally promise myself to never do it again.

"All right," he says. "Go on back up front and finish setting up."

I nod and rejoin Em.

"Unbelievable," I say in a low voice when I'm within earshot of her.

"What?" she asks.

"I'm going to totally kill Daisy when I see her. She told Derek that I'm giving away free drinks to my friends."

"Omigod, what a witch!" Em says. She stops refilling the cookie tray to look at me.

"Yeah, I can't believe she'd do that to me," I say. I twist my hair with my fingers.

"Especially when I've seen her giving away low-fat muffins to her Jazzercise friends!" Em says.

"Jazzercise?" I giggle at the thought of Daisy dancing around a room with a bunch of women. "Yeah, I guess I can see that."

"Well, I know why she did it," Em says.

"Why?"

"She wants your job."

"Really?"

"Uh-huh. Daisy thought she should have been promoted to assistant manager."

"Why? I'm totally better than her and I've been here longer," I say.

Em shrugs.

"What a brat."

"You definitely have to put her in her place," Em says.

"I will," I agree. "For starters, I think someone should be on bathroom cleaning duty for at least the next month."

Em nods and gives me a thumbs-up.

By five-twenty a.m., we're ready to open up the store.

"You still haven't asked me about Cam," Em says.

"I'm sorry, I meant to. What's going on?"

"Well," she tells me, her eyes lighting up, "he's taking me roller skating tonight! Can you imagine? I haven't been roller skating since I was like ten."

I smile. "That is so cute."

"Then he wants to go to a fifties restaurant for cheeseburgers and milkshakes."

"It sounds like you guys will totally have fun."

"Seriously, Jane," Em says, refilling the stack of cups by the register, "I didn't think this was a good idea at all, what with the whole Jason thing, but it has really made me feel better! And Cam is awesome. You are such a great Espressologist!"

"A what?" Derek appears behind us, fastening an apron around his back, preparing to help us with the expected crowd.

"Oh, um . . ." Em stammers, looking back and forth between Derek and me.

"Nothing?" I offer.

"No, I heard you guys. You said Jane is 'a great Espressologist.' What did you mean? What is an Espressologist?" I look down at the floor, shaking my head slightly, indicating to Em that I want her to keep her mouth shut. Em glances at me and then looks back at Derek.

"I'll tell you but you can't get mad at Jane. Because it's totally a cool thing."

"Em!" I warn.

"What's the big deal, Jane? It is so cool," she says.

"Now you are making me nervous. Start talking," Derek says.

"Well, like I said, it's really awesome," Em begins, and I sigh heavily, trying to prepare for another verbal lashing from Derek. "Jane has been keeping this notebook for a really long time. She records all the drinks people order and what type of person they are. It's kind of like she's typecasting people based on their coffee preference or something."

I inwardly recoil, closing my eyes and remembering how I had lied and told Derek my notebook was for my notes on drinks for the "Assistant Manager's Specialty Drink of the Week." I open one eye, turn my head, and glance at Derek. He's staring at me, obviously remembering our conversation. Crap, crap, crap.

"Now wait," Em says, seeing Derek starting to look huffy, "don't get mad yet. Here's the cool part. Jane calls it Espressology and she's been matchmaking people based on it!"

"Matchmaking people? Matchmaking whom?" Derek demands.

"Well, customers and staff mostly," Em says, now slowing down the story as she realizes Derek is less than pleased with the information.

"You are matchmaking now? While you're working?" Derek asks, looking at me.

"Well, yeah, a little," I mumble.

"But she's amazing, Derek, I swear," Em interrupts. "She's dead-on each time. It's totally crazy. Simone and Gavin, Sarah and the cop, Cam and me . . . it's really cool."

Derek is still staring at me and I can't tell what he is thinking. Em knows that she is getting me in trouble and can't stop talking.

"Derek, seriously, you can't bloody well get mad at Jane. It has no negative effect on the store. I mean, if anything, it is improving business," she continues, waving her hands in the air. "Everyone wants to be in love and she's making it happen. She's making people totally happy and they love her for it. They are coming in even more for coffee. It's a good thing! Really . . ." She trails off, and there is dead silence as we wait for Derek to say something.

Derek slumps against the sink with his arms crossed. His face is scrunched up like he's thinking hard, and he stares straight ahead at nothing in particular. I have no idea what he's going to do next. He wouldn't fire me over this, would he? Well, he could. He's caught me lying, oh, I don't know, how many times now? Em is giving me a worried look. She mouths, "I'm sorry." We both wait for Derek's tirade to begin. About twenty of the longest seconds on earth pass and then the corners of Derek's lips turn up a bit.

"I'll be right back," he says, walking away from us.

"Em!" I scream when I'm sure he is out of the room. "How could you do that to me?"

"I know, I know, I'm so sorry. I was just happy. And talking too much. And I really didn't think he'd get mad. I mean, c'mon, what's the big deal?"

I shake my head and frown. "What do you think he's doing back there?"

"I don't know. I'm really, really sorry, Jane."

"Do you think he's going to fire me on the spot? Maybe he's getting my last check?" I ask.

"No, he'd be so screwed if he fired you. It's Black Friday and we're about to open."

"Still," I say.

"Jane, if he fires you, then I walk, too, and he's MAJORLY screwed. Let him serve the crazed Elmo 5000 seekers all by himself," she declares.

"Really?"

"Yeah, it's totally my fault. I'm positive he won't fire you."

Just then Derek rejoins us up front with a piece of paper in his hands. Oh god, I think, this is it. He's giving me some kind of termination paper. He hands me the piece of paper. I take a deep breath and look down.

"What's this?" It says THE ESPRESSOLOGIST IS IN. "I don't get it."

"You are our holiday promotion," he says enthusiastically.

"I don't get it," I repeat.

"It's simple. Corporate says I need to do a promotion to

bring in more customers over the holiday season, and you, my little Espressologist, are it." I glance back and forth from Derek to Em trying to take in what he just told me. Derek walks over to the front glass door and unlocks it, letting the ten or so waiting customers in to start screaming drink orders at us.

Ho, ho, freakin' ho to me.

8

Class, settle down, settle down," Professor Monroe says as she stands up and walks to the front of her desk. "I'm going to pass out your biographies from last week and then we are going to talk about your final papers." She begins to walk around the room, returning papers, as Cam bolts through the door and slips into his seat behind me.

"Hey, Cam!" I turn around in my seat and grin at him. "I was wondering if you were going to make it."

"Did she notice I'm late?" Cam asks, nodding at Professor Monroe.

"Not at all. She's just handing back last week's paper. Which you are of course going to let me read, right?"

"Hmm, I don't know," he teases. "Maybe on the last day of class. Then you can't get mad at me, decide you are never talking to me again, and act all awkward each time you see me in class."

"Cam! What the heck did you write that would make me never talk to you again? Now you have to let me see it."

"Nope. Last day."

I pout a little. "Well, you can't read yours either, then," I say.

"All right."

"What, don't you want to read it? Aren't you curious?"

"No, not really."

Guys suck so bad sometimes. Cam turns to his left, reaches down, and rifles through his bag looking for something. As he is doing this, Professor Monroe slips his paper onto his desk from his right. I try to read it upside down as fast as I can. Cam glances up, sees what I am doing, and snaps back upright, covering the paper with his hand.

"Uh-uh," he says, shaking his head and smiling at me. "Not today."

I glare at him and turn around quickly in my seat. I didn't see much, but I did catch a few words of the paper. Something about me being "weak" and "timid." How dare he!

Professor Monroe spends the rest of the class period going over our final assignment, but I don't really pay attention. The words *weak* and *timid* keep going through my mind. Is that what Cam really thinks of me? I thought he was my friend. I thought he was such a good guy. Maybe he isn't right for Em after all. Maybe I was totally wrong about him.

The class ends and I gather my stuff and head for the door.

"Jane, wait," Cam calls.

"Later. I have to get to work." I put on my gloves and pull my coat tight around me. I walk out the double doors of Anthony Carter Community College and start the short three-block walk to work in the freezing cold.

ᴄᴇ✦ᴏᴏ

A few minutes later I walk into Wired Joe's. I am instantly bummed to see that none of the people I like are working today. Though I should have already known that, since Derek showed me the schedule earlier in the week. Ever since this whole Espressologist thing came up I haven't been able to think straight.

Daisy and Brenda are standing behind the counter taking orders and making drinks. Brenda gives me a fake smile but Daisy only glares. Great, fun afternoon ahead, I think. Daisy is pissy with me because a) she didn't get me in trouble with Derek last week and b) she's been getting really comfy with the smell of toilet bowl cleaner since I've designated her the spinner for whenever we are working together. This means every fifteen minutes or so Daisy has to check the bathrooms, bus the tables, clean and stock the condiment bar, and make sure everything looks good throughout the store.

On the other hand, Brenda, our store's official chalkboard artist, is a little annoyed because Derek asked her to come up with a fantastic sign to post on Fridays to advertise my talents.

I quickly put my things away, tie on my apron, and join the girls up front.

"Oh good, you're ready," Brenda says. "Now you can take over up here so I can go sit and work on *your* sign." She practically snarls the words at me like I've done something wrong. I'm no happier about this than she is. In fact, worrying about it all week is giving me an ulcer, I think. Brenda disappears to get her supplies and returns to the front in moments. She stops momentarily by me at the register. "So what is this"— she points at the board—"all about, anyway?"

I sigh. "Well," I begin, "long story short, I'm the new Friday night attraction. From six to ten on Friday nights I will be taking down drink orders and matchmaking. It's called Espressology."

"Does it work?" she asks.

"Yeah." I can see Daisy out of the corner of my eye looking at me like I'm full of it.

"Why haven't we ever heard of this before?" Daisy asks with an attitude.

"Because I haven't told you about it," I snap. I'm so not in the mood for any crap from Daisy today. "Have you checked the bathrooms recently?" Daisy makes a face and leaves the counter to go on toilet duty.

While I'm busily glaring at Daisy's retreating back, the door swings open and my dad walks in. I quickly look at

Brenda and shake my head a little as I eye the chalkboard. I do NOT want my parents to find out about this Espressology stuff. Not yet, at least. We have a fairly easy, stress-free child-parent relationship going on these days and I don't want to rock it.

"How's my favorite barista?" he says, approaching the counter.

"Good, Dad." I love it when my dad comes in. Not only is he a friendly face, but he always leaves a ten-dollar bill in the tip jar. "Small cappuccino?"

"Is she good or what?" he asks Brenda.

Brenda laughs. "She's good." She retreats to a nearby table with her supplies, still close enough to overhear our conversation.

I ring up his order and make his drink. When I turn around I see a ten in the tip jar. Dad is so dependable.

He takes a sip of his drink. "Mmm, tastes great," he says loudly to the store. Like I need extra help selling this stuff. "See you at home, sweetie," he says, just to me.

"Bye, Dad." I watch him leave.

"Your dad is so cute," Brenda says.

"Yeah." I pause. "You know, my mom and dad fell in love over coffee, so maybe it was my destiny to bring others together through my Espressology."

"Deep." Brenda giggles.

I give her a wounded look.

"No really, it does actually sound kind of cool," Brenda

says. "I don't work Friday night, but I might have to come in and check it out."

"Sure," I say, grateful for the small bit of kindness. I want her to think I have everything under control, but inside I'm totally freaking out. Friday is only two days away. What if I look like a gigantic moron? What if I can't in fact really do this? So what if I matched three couples? It could be a total fluke. Nevertheless, I've been studying my notebook every night since Derek told me I'd have to start playing Espressologist this Friday. I even skipped studying for my chemistry quiz to study my Espressology. Derek said that each Friday he's going to set up the huge chalkboard outside, with the words:

The Espressologist is In
Fridays 6–10 p.m.
Come in for a little latte and love

The plan is that from six to ten I'll sit at a small table in the front of the store near where the drink orders are taken. People who want to participate will give me their phone numbers or e-mail addresses and I'll jot down notes on them and their drink orders into a spreadsheet on my laptop. They can hang around and see if I match them sometime during the four hours, or I can have their coffee match call or e-mail them. The service is free; well, after the customers buy a drink, that is. I'm totally freaking out because I've never had to do this on demand before. I mean, it has all just been for fun so far. And what if my matches are just a huge coincidence and I am in fact 100 percent full of crap with my coffee theory? Ugh. I just have to stop thinking about it.

೩ა৯

I'm busily making six small white chocolate mochas for a moms' club meeting when my already bad day gets even worse. Melissa and Ginny are heading into the store.

"Jane!" Melissa exclaims happily, striding up to the counter. "Isn't December fantastic? I just love that adorable holiday music you have playing in here."

I give her a wary look.

"What can I get you guys?" I ask in a flat voice.

"Did I mention that I ran into Jane 'off hours,'" Melissa says to Ginny, making dramatic air quotes with her fingers, "a couple of weeks ago?"

"No, where?" Ginny asks.

I stare at both of them with my mouth hanging slightly open. Do they even see me? Hello, running a business here. *Place your orders already,* I beam at them with my eyes.

"Oh, here of course." Melissa laughs. "But she wasn't working. She was on a date!"

"Really . . ." Ginny raises her eyebrows and looks from Melissa to me.

I clear my throat. "Like I said before, what can I get you guys?"

Melissa completely ignores my question. "Yeah, and he was a total hottie, too! I didn't see any family resemblance." At this, they both erupt in laughter.

"That's enough!" I say loud enough that most of the other customers turn to look at us. "From now on we are going to just keep our exchanges to coffee, got it?" I'm shaking a little bit—surprised at myself for being able to be so direct with Melissa.

"What? I don't understand." Melissa looks slightly wounded. "I thought we were friends."

"What?" I spit at her. "When were *we* friends?"

"Well, uh . . ." she stammers.

"Yeah, let me help you out," I say in a much quieter voice. "We never were and we never will be. Now place your order, give me your money, and go wait for your drink." Melissa stares at me for a moment with a stunned expression on her face.

"Two small nonfat lattes," she whispers, sliding me her credit card. I roughly mark two cups with their drink orders, ring them up, and quickly make the drinks. I keep the same mean face on until I watch the two girls leave the store with their drinks. As soon as the door closes behind them I fall back against the sink, shaking. I cover my mouth with one hand. I can't believe I just did that. I finally told that witch off. I handled her all by myself without Em whooshing in to save me. I have got to call Em right now and tell her all about it.

⟡

It's about an hour before closing and we're doing our nightly cleanup. Brenda is mopping the floors, Daisy is hauling the garbage out back, and I'm handling the counter by myself when Will walks in alone. I'm a little surprised to see him in here this late, but I had already thought about our next meeting and had decided to play it really cool with him about the whole Thanksgiving thing. Will gives me a huge grin.

"Hello," I say plainly. "What can I get you?"

"The usual."

"Really?" I can't resist asking. "It's kind of late."

"Yeah, I have a late night ahead of me."

I nod. "That will be three fifty."

Will looks puzzled. "What?"

"That will be three fifty," I repeat.

"Oh," he says, slowly pulling out his wallet, not taking his eyes off of me. I keep a straight face, but I want to laugh at his reaction to actually having to pay for his coffee. I ring him up and start to make his drink. Will comes around to the pick-up counter and watches me work. "So," he begins.

"So," I echo, quickly pulling shots and dumping them into his waiting cup.

"I was really bummed you weren't able to make it on Thanksgiving."

What?! What the heck is he talking about?

"Excuse me?" I say.

"You know, Thanksgiving. You said you were going to try to come over for our little celebration. I guess you couldn't get out of your family thing."

I hesitate with the ice scooper in my hand, trying to figure out the best way to respond to this.

"No, I couldn't make it. I had dinner with my family and then I met up with a few people." There. That sounds kind of good. At least I don't sound pathetic.

"Yeah, I figured something like that happened," he says.

Yeah, right.

"But I did try to leave you a voice mail to let you know I wasn't coming," I add, not wanting to just let the whole phone-turned-off thing go.

"Really? I didn't get it."

"Yeah, your phone wasn't in service or something."

"What?" he says, taking his phone out, flipping it open, and looking at it like it is going to tell him what happened on Thanksgiving or something. "What number did you dial?"

Okay, it's sad I know, but I have the phone number he gave me in my apron.

I pretend to think. "You know, I think it might still be in my pocket somewhere." I feel around in them, first the left and then the right, and produce a crumpled piece of paper. "Ah, here it is." I smooth it down on the table. Will looks at it.

"I'm such an idiot."

"Why?"

"I got the numbers mixed up. I reversed the last two digits. It's a new phone." He holds his hands up in a "what can you do?" manner. "I'm such an idiot," he repeats.

"No, you're not," I say, with one hundred times more enthusiasm than I had a few moments ago. It was a mistake. He wasn't trying to get rid of me.

"Forgive me for being such a dunce," he says. "Maybe we'll try to do it again sometime?" Will takes his drink and heads toward the door.

"Sure," I say, watching his beautiful backside walk out of Wired Joe's.

9

It's really here. Espressology night. I've been standing outside in the cold staring at the huge chalkboard announcing tonight's activities for a good five minutes. I have to admit, Brenda did a fantastic job. The board looks amazing. All red and white and silvery dust swirling around the edges. I'm clutching my Espressology notebook and my laptop to my chest. Derek pops his head out the door.

"Coming in or what?"

"Mmm-hmm," I mumble, not moving an inch. Derek steps outside, grabs both of my shoulders from behind, and gently pushes me toward the door. I guess in all the excitement he forgot about his no-touching rule.

"Come on," he says. "It's freezing out here."

I let him guide me into the store and to the back. The warm air makes my cheeks burn a little bit.

"You look scared to death," he observes once we are in his office and he's closed the door. I take a seat in the chair opposite his.

"Pretty much," I admit. And I'm not kidding—I've had a sick stomach all afternoon.

"Well, take your coat and gloves off and relax a minute. Gather your thoughts. It's going to be fun," Derek assures me.

It is really strange having Derek be nice to me. Completely out of the ordinary for him. He must really need me to do this.

"I have a table set up in front of the registers with a red velvet tablecloth over it and a rose in a vase. When you are ready, go have a seat and do your thing."

"You went all out," I say.

"This is going to be big, I think. People have been talking about it all day."

"Really?" Now I feel even more bolted to the chair I'm sitting on.

"Yeah, sales are already up today just from people stopping in to ask what an Espressologist is."

"Wow," I mutter.

"Here, I got you this to wear." Derek hands me a cute red apron with the Wired Joe's logo embroidered on it in shiny silver. The name tag hanging off it says ESPRESSOLOGIST at the top, and then my name directly underneath. It has a tiny cupid in the corner.

"Holy crap," I say, "you are serious about this."

"Dead. Now get yourself together, come on out, and let's make a lot of money."

I nod and Derek heads out front. I slip the red apron over my black turtleneck and black skirt and I have to admit, it looks pretty cute. I stand up, do a quick hair check, and head to my post.

I trek up front feeling like a freshman communications student getting ready to give a speech for the first time to the entire school, but there really aren't that many people out there. Yeah, it is a little busier than usual, but there are only about five people in line. They all look at me eagerly, though, so I know they are waiting for me. Sarah and Frankie, one of our newer baristas, are making drinks at the bar, and Daisy is working at the register.

"Here she is, everyone," Derek booms to the entire store. "Our local Espressologist, Jane. Give your coffee drink order to one of our baristas at the register and then step over to Jane and tell her your favorite drink. Jane will take down your information and find your perfect love match for the holidays. She has never been wrong. Just step right up and give it a try."

Geez, where is your top hat, Derek? He sounds like he is introducing a circus act. Okay, deep breath, deep breath. I can do this.

I smile and give a little wave to the people in line. "Hey, everyone. Just gimme a minute to get organized." I put my notebook down on the tablecloth and place my laptop right next to it. I flip it open and give the power button a slight push. I set it on standby before I left home, so it only takes a moment to turn on and for my spreadsheet to appear. The spreadsheet was Em's idea. She thought it would help if I had all the information I needed already in a table so I wouldn't blank and forget what to ask. She actually made the spreadsheet for me last night when she came over. She said she was there to help me relax about the whole Espressology thing today, but I know she just wanted to talk about Cam. She thinks she's all in *love* with him now. How can she be in love with him already? Puh-lease. They've only been on two dates, but she says she can just tell he is so perfect for her. I thought he was perfect for her, too, but strictly in the just-for-fun, not-falling-in-love kind of way. I mean, my god, she just broke up with her long-term boyfriend. She can't move on this fast, can she?

I've got to stop thinking about Em and Cam and concentrate on what is happening right here before Derek kills me. He's standing about three feet away just staring at me. Like I'm going to wave a wand and alakazam, couples will skip out the door arm in arm. There is a little more to Espressology than that. I reread my table headings on my spreadsheet: name, sex, age, coffee, interesting tidbit, phone, e-mail, match.

"Ready," I say, mustering a cheery voice. "Who's first?"

"I am." A nervous, slightly overweight woman in a bright red fleece jacket steps toward me. She has on matching bright red lipstick, long fake red nails, and heavy eye makeup. Definitely a real estate agent. I can almost smell the pack of cigarettes undoubtedly in her giant purse and sense her newer model Caddy parked in the garage around the corner. "Who am I supposed to talk to?" she asks.

I smile. "Well, just tell your order to the barista behind the register so she can start your drink. You'll pay her and then come over and chat with me while one of the other baristas makes it."

"Okay." She looks from Daisy to me and back to Daisy. She clears her voice and says loudly, "I want a caramel-flavored mack-a-cheeto in the big cup. And with skim milk, please." She gives us both a pleased look, obviously proud she could remember her order.

"Large nonfat caramel macchiato," Daisy says loudly, and marks the cup. She hands it to Sarah, who starts the drink.

"What? What did you say?" the woman says, looking slightly panicked. Obviously she doesn't come into Wired Joe's too often.

"Don't worry, she's just giving your order to the other barista," I assure her. "Now we chat."

The woman lets out a slight giggle of relief as she pays Daisy and steps in front of me. "Oh, okay," she says. "Usually, I just get my caramel mack-a-cheetos at the drive-through Wired Joe's near my house. They never yell the order at me." She glares at Daisy just for a moment.

I nod.

"Let me just get down some information, then. Name?"

"Debbie. Debbie Archer."

"Hi, Debbie. Age? And you can just give me a ballpark here if you don't want to tell me."

"Late thirties," she says.

Riiiiiight.

"All right." I enter what she told me. "Now just tell me some interesting tidbit about you so I can get a better feel for who you are."

The "interesting tidbit" category was also Em's idea. She thought if the customers told me a little funny something about themselves, it would help me remember them later on when I'm doing matches.

"Well, I'm searching hard for my soul mate. I've done it all, personal ads, online dating, you name it. But I still haven't found *him*. Sometimes I think I'll never find my soul mate."

I can't help but feel touched at this woman's honesty. I type, "Searching for soul mate" into my spreadsheet.

"Now just give me your phone number and e-mail address and if I find your match tonight or in the near future I'll have him get in touch with you."

She gives me her contact info, thanks me, and heads out into the night, caramel macchiato in hand.

"Next," I say. Three young teenage girls are huddled close together and whispering. The shortest girl gives their order quietly to Daisy and slides her some money and then they all eye me up and down. Do I even need to ask? Obviously it is going to be frappycaps all around.

The tallest girl steps out to the front and holds her hand

out like she's carrying a serving tray. She has her blond hair pulled into a loose ponytail and she's wearing three different-colored tight shirts in layers, skinny jeans tucked into purple slouch boots, and a long dark purple coat.

"Well, I'm Sadie and my favorite drink is a small vanilla-bean frappycap. This here is Jenna," she says, pointing to a shorter girl with dark hair, camouflage pants, a camouflage army hat, and a zipped black puffy jacket. "And this"—she indicates the last girl who has short brown hair, a Mexico team soccer jacket, a red T-shirt, and jeans—"is Izzie. They both like small strawberries-and-crème frappycaps."

I inwardly smile and type. They kind of remind me of Em, Katie, Ava, and me freshman year.

"Okay, guys, ages?"

"We're fourteen," Jenna answers shyly.

"And our interesting tidbit," Izzie pipes in, "is that we are all Guild Masters in *World of Warcraft*."

"Impressive," I say, although I'm not really sure what they are talking about. Obviously some kind of video game. I enter their information. This is actually kind of fun. The girls take their drinks to a table near the door to hang out.

After I finish typing, I look up and see the sweetest-looking older gentleman. He's got to be in his late sixties. He's bald and wearing a dark brown corduroy golf hat, a thick brown peacoat, and a red-and-black plaid scarf. He totally looks like the university professor type.

"I'd like a short cappuccino," he says in a deep, booming

voice to Daisy, and then faces me. I've already started typing his drink choice into my spreadsheet.

He *is* smart. I knew it. And money-conscious. Not many people order the short cappuccino, since it isn't actually on the menu. It's eight ounces and cheaper than the twelve-ounce small, which is the smallest size that we advertise, but it has the same amount of espresso in it. He's getting more bang for his buck.

Gregory—that's the name he gives me—steps over to my table and provides the required info, but I'm hardly listening. I already know the PERFECT match for him. These two completely adorable sisters, Belinda and Anna, also in their sixties, come into our store every Sunday morning before they head off for their weekly grocery shopping trip. I nicknamed them "the bargain babes" because they order the same thing every week: a doppio on ice, which is basically two shots of espresso over ice. Then they take their cups over to the milk station, where they fill them up the rest of the way with the free milk we have out. Voilà, iced lattes for almost two dollars less than the menu price. I happen to know that Belinda is a retired librarian and a widow. I type "Belinda?" in the match box in Gregory's row and make a mental note to talk to her on Sunday. I'm so excited—I can do this! I can match perfect strangers.

I'm super happy with myself and looking forward to my next customer. Just then three young boys with long dark shaggy hair and glasses, wearing long-sleeve tees and droopy pants, come in through the door. Something about them just screams future software developers to me. I'm struck with inspiration and whip around in my chair to see if the teenage girls are still there. They are. Could this be my first on-the-spot match? Okay, calm down. Let's see what they order first.

One of the boys steps up to the counter and gives Daisy his order. He turns to me and says, "Hey. I'm Ed. This is James and this is Dan. We ordered three small hot chocolates. That's our favorite drink."

BINGO. I don't even have to check my notebook to know they are a match with the girls.

I take down their information, for record's sake, and wait for them to get their hot chocolates. I open a new document and peck furiously at random keys, just to look busy for a few minutes. Even though I already know their perfect matches, I don't want them to know it was so easy. There. Enough time has passed. I get up and Derek comes whipping around from behind the coffee bean display where he's been hovering and says, "Hey, where are you going?"

I wink. "Gimme a minute." I walk over to the boys' table, take Ed and James by the arm, and indicate with a nod for Dan to follow us. I lead them to the table near the door where the girls are sitting. "Sadie, Jenna, and Izzie," I say, "meet Ed, James, and Dan." All six of the teenagers act awkward for a moment, but then James sees Jenna's PSP sitting out on the table and slides into a chair next to her and asks her what game she's playing.

My work here is done.

I hurry back toward my table and pause by Derek with my hand in the air waiting for a high five. He glares at me like I was just picking my nose and shoves both of his hands into his pockets.

"What was that about?" he asks.

"I made my first match. Well, actually my first three matches," I say with an enormous smile on my face. Yes!

10

It was so much fun, Em, seriously. Awesome. I made eight matches last night alone. EIGHT MATCHES! And there is potential for at least four more." I'm sitting cross-legged on Em's bed recounting the evening's events. Em is searching through her backpack for her history notes.

"Shoot! Shoot, shoot, shoot!" Em says, throwing her backpack on the floor.

"Everything okay?"

"Not really. I'm dead if I don't find my history notes. There is an exam on Monday and it's worth half our grade." Em sits down in her chair and puts her head on her desk.

"Well, relax. Just call someone from class, borrow their notes for an hour, and run over to the library and make a copy."

"Hmm . . ." she says, standing up and looking at me.

"That could work. Okay. Wow. I feel much better. Thanks!"

"No prob; now back to me."

"I'm sorry!" Em laughs and plops down on the bed next to me. "Go ahead, tell me more about the big Espressology night."

"It was fun. I mean really, really fun. I didn't think I'd have such a good time. I'm totally made for this."

"That's so cool," she says. "See? I knew you could do it."

"Yeah, and Derek was stoked. It was our busiest Friday night ever. I swear he would have kissed me if he didn't hate all people."

"I'm happy for you, Jane, really. I'm happy that good things are happening for both of us."

Both of us? Oh god, is she going to talk about Cam again?

"Yeah," I agree, bracing myself for what I know is coming next.

"I can't believe how awesome Cam is, Jane. Thanks again for setting us up."

"Sure," I say flatly.

"He's made me forget about Jason. I mean totally. Jason even called me the other day wanting to talk. I asked him who it was and he was all, 'You mean you forgot my voice already?' and I said, 'Seriously, who is this?' I could tell he was hurt and I'm glad."

"Ooh . . . drama! Well, having another guy to date is totally good for revenge on Jason."

"But Cam isn't revenge, Jane. I really like him."

"Yeah, you keep saying that."

"What?" Em stands up and stomps over to her dresser for her bottle of water. "You don't believe me?"

"Oh no, I believe you. I guess I'm just shocked. Shocked at how fast you moved on," I say.

"That's a good thing, though, isn't it?" she demands.

"I guess it is," I answer. Maybe if I agree, she'll just drop the whole conversation.

"Well, hey, maybe we can double soon? You can ask Will out and the four of us can do something," Em says.

I'm not sure why, but the thought of going on a double date with Em and Cam sounds about as fun as a colon cleansing. Which I've never experienced, but my mom says it is super gross.

"Um, I don't know about Will," I say.

"Why? I thought you guys cleared everything up."

"We did. I'm just not sure if it is in the beans for us. I'll have to check my notebook," I tell her.

"Jaaaane!" Em sings, laughing. "Freaking make it in the beans, girl. Change your favorite drink if you have to."

"Uh! I can't just *make* our drinks match. This is serious stuff, Em!"

Em shakes her head and reaches for the phone to hunt down those history notes.

෧ৄঌ

"Love is in the air." I sigh, happily restacking a pile of coupons on the counter at work. Brenda is on the other side of the pick-up table, wiping it down.

"That was too cute," she agrees.

The store has been pretty slow for a Tuesday afternoon, except for this adorable couple who just got engaged. The girl said that her boyfriend picked her up from work for "lunch" and brought her down to the rocks by the lake. It was totally freezing, so she had no idea what they were doing there. Then he got on one knee and proposed. She said yes and they played hooky from work for the rest of the afternoon. They just came in for medium mocha cappuccinos for here. I drew a heart with chocolate syrup on top of the foam in each of their mugs.

"How is the best assistant manager ever?" Derek asks, setting a stack of papers on the counter while he slips on his jacket. He's getting ready to leave for the day.

"Are you talking to me?" I say, wide-eyed.

"Who else?"

He gives me an ear-to-ear grin.

"You're in a fantastic mood," I say.

"That I am. I just got off the phone with our district manager. He said our promotion is fantastic and to keep up the great work. We did more sales than any other Wired Joe's in the district last Friday! Can you believe it?"

"Omigod! No, not really. That's insane! I mean, I knew it was busy but . . . wow."

"'We've got to really advertise all week and get people extra pumped up for this Friday. I want us to beat last week's sales."

No pressure or anything.

"How are the matches going?" he asks.

"Great. I'm at eleven matched couples right now. All of them have either instant-messaged, e-mailed, or chatted on the phone. Three of the couples have already had their first date. I've been getting some really positive e-mails back from the couples all week."

"Seriously?" Derek gets excited all over again. "That's fantastic, Jane! Can you get some positive quotes from your matched couples so I can put them up around the store to advertise this Friday's event?"

"Sure. I don't think it will be a problem. I'll ask a couple of them and get back to you."

"Excellent job, Jane!" Derek says, pointing his index finger at me as he heads out of the store. "Don't be surprised if you get a raise soon."

Though I've never seen anyone other than a cartoon person do this, I half expect him to do one of those sideways heel clicks in the air as he walks away.

"Cool!" I reply, feeling all smiley. I can't believe how my luck is changing.

Seconds after Derek leaves, the door swings open and Melissa and Ginny enter. How does this chick continually sense my happiness and swoop in to squash it? Well, at least she should behave this time after our last talk.

"Hello," I greet them in a professional voice. "The usual?"

"Oh, *wow,*" Melissa exclaims, "are we considered regulars now? That is so cute—just like that old show *Cheers.*"

Ginny giggles.

"Yes, Jane, get us *the usual,*" Melissa says with great dramatic flair.

I sigh and inwardly roll my eyes. What a twit. I run her credit card through the machine, mark their cups, and push them toward Brenda to make.

"So, Gin," Melissa starts, "can you believe our little Jane is an Espressologist?"

"A what?" Ginny asks.

"An Espressologist. My friend Michelle from my textiles class told me all about it. Jane is matchmaking people via their coffee choices every Friday night. She even matched Michelle last week."

"Really?" Ginny looks from Melissa to me and back to Melissa.

"Yeah. Jane's future may not have appeared too promising in school last year, but I always had hope for her. I knew she'd do something really big," Melissa continues.

Is she being legit? Have we actually turned a corner since our big confrontation? Can we move on from all this? Can we actually even be friends?

"Yeah, I heard she dumps out your used espresso grounds onto a table and talks to them. They tell her who your future spouse is. She's like a carny fortune-teller or something.

Whooooooo!" she says, wiggling her fingers in the air at Ginny.

Or then again, maybe Melissa is still the same big-mouth idiot she always has been.

"That is not what I do," I say angrily. "There is an actual science to it."

"Didn't you get D's in science?" She laughs.

How did she know that? What, did she get a hold of my transcripts?

"Tell you what," I offer, "come in Friday and I'll show you. I'll match you with someone."

"Me?" she asks. "You want to match me? Ha! No thanks. I can certainly find my own dates."

"Fine." I shrug. "Suit yourself. Looks like your drinks are up."

Brenda calls out, "Small nonfat lattes."

Melissa grabs her drink and Ginny looks at me like she's going to add something.

"C'mon, Gin," Melissa says, and Ginny follows her out the door.

11

This is a nice surprise. What did I do to earn an escort to class?" I ask.

Em and I are powerwalking up West Jackson Boulevard on the way to my English class at the college.

"I have a pass to go to the college library and do some research for a paper, so I thought I'd just keep you company for a few," Em replies.

Ha. Yeah, right. She knows Cam is in my English class. I'm sure she just wants to "bump" into him.

"Thanks. You're a sweetie. So, did I tell you the latest with Will?" I can barely keep the excitement out of my voice.

"No, you didn't. Tell me, tell me," she says.

"He came in last night and was totally flirting."

"Obviously."

"No, really, I didn't know what to expect. I know he

explained away the whole Thanksgiving thing, but I wasn't sure if I believed him or not. But now I do. He's so cute," I say.

"And cute boys never lie. Kidding!" she exclaims when I scowl at her.

"Like everyone else who came in yesterday, he wanted to talk to me about the whole Espressology thing."

"Of course," she says, grabbing my arm and steering me around a homeless guy sitting in front of a building and yelling at people to give him money.

"He looked deep into my eyes and told me he was lonely and really hoped he could find love, too. He totally had me in a trance. I could hardly talk," I tell her.

"No way. What did you do?"

"I told him to stop in on Friday night and I'd see what I could do," I say.

"Cool! I work this Friday night, too. So is he coming?"

"Uh, no."

"Why not?"

"Some fraternity thing. But he promised to come in next Friday. I told him we are only doing this for four weeks," I say.

"You are going to match him with you, right?"

"Duh. Of course. But I feel kind of bad about it."

"Why in the world would you feel bad about it?"

"Because I checked my notebook and we are not exactly a match."

"Rough," Em says.

"I know, but he *has* to be mine. I'll just have to fudge this one."

"Definitely," Em agrees as we approach the door to my school.

"This is me."

"Um, okay." She looks up and down the sidewalk. I can tell she's looking for Cam. "Are you working tonight?"

"You already asked me that," I reply. "Are you okay?"

Just then Cam turns the corner and heads straight for us.

"Hi, Cam," Em says dreamily.

Cam opens his mouth to respond.

"I'll leave you two to talk," I announce before he can say anything. I really don't need to hear any lovey-dovey gush between those two. I head into the school and toward my classroom.

❧

I take my seat and shrug off my jacket. Although I don't want to, I'm thinking about Cam and Em and wondering what they are talking about outside. I don't have long to think, though, because Cam comes in only a minute or so later and slides into his seat behind me.

"Hey," he says.

"Hey." I briefly glance back at him.

"How's it going?"

"Not bad," I answer, still facing forward.

"Can you turn around?" he asks.

I want to stay mad at him for what he wrote in his biography of me, but it is hard. I turn around.

"Yes?" I ask.

"Hey," he says again.

"Hey," I say again.

"I just wanted to see you smile," he tells me, and my heart defrosts like thirty degrees. "Last day of class, huh?"

"I know," I reply. "Did you get your final paper done?"

"Yeah, you?" he asks.

"Barely. It's been a crazy week."

"So I hear."

What exactly did he hear? I wonder. Does Em talk about me to him? Oh god, they have this whole separate relationship and they talk about me!

It's silent for a moment, and we are just looking at each other. A tuft of his shaggy blond hair is almost over his right eye, and I suddenly have the urge to brush it back for him. But I resist. It's not nice to brush back other people's boyfriends' hair. Especially not your best friend's boyfriend.

"Do you remember what I said you could do on the last day?" he asks.

I sit for a moment thinking. "No . . ."

He reaches into his folder and pulls out some stapled sheets. "I said you could read the paper I wrote on you."

"Oh, no thanks," I say, suddenly feeling a little angry again.

"Aren't you curious?" He looks at me with a puzzled expression.

"No. Why would I be?" I lie.

Cam lays the paper faceup on his desk and shrugs. "Okay. That's fine." He scribbles something in the corner of the paper and his pencil breaks. "Shoot. Be right back." He stands and walks to the pencil sharpener near the door.

I can't help it. I grab the paper and flip to the last page, last paragraph, and read as fast as possible.

If there was one thing Jane could use more of, it's confidence. Because everyone else can see what Jane doesn't see—she's much smarter, stronger, and more beautiful than she realizes. And that is just a matter of time, because when she does, the Melissas of the world had better watch out.

Huh? Cam thinks I'm beautiful? Leave it to me to jump right to that. He said I was other stuff, too. Out of the corner of my eye I see Cam begin to turn away from the pencil sharpener and I quickly shut his paper. I can feel my face flush.

Cam sits down at his desk and cocks his head. "Everything all right?"

"Um, yeah. Sure." I glance down at the paper. Oh, crap. It's turned a good forty-five degrees farther to the left than how Cam had it. Does he notice?

"You look like you want to say something."

"No, not really." Except do you really think the things you wrote in your paper about me being strong and smart and stuff? But I can't exactly say that.

I turn around as Professor Monroe comes in and tosses her briefcase on her desk. I look at Cam once more. "I just wanted to say that I'm really happy for you and Em. I'm glad you guys found each other. It must be nice to have such a special connection with someone."

Cam's eyebrows scrunch up, and he's got that weird, wounded look on his face again, like that day we were at Wired Joe's working on our papers.

"I hope I find love someday, too," I add.

Nice. Now I'm just babbling. Somebody turn me off! I quickly face the front and close my eyes. Darn. That love thing was going too far, wasn't it? What if he and Em haven't exchanged the three big words yet? She'll be pissed. I can feel Cam staring at the back of my head, but there is no way I'm turning around again for the rest of class.

12

Oh. My. God!" I say, gripping the door handle of Katie's car. Katie said she wanted to see the whole Espressology thing in action and offered to pick me up and bring me to work. She lets out a low whistle next to me.

"Holy crap," she utters in a quiet voice.

We are both staring at the line of people wrapped around the corner at Wired Joe's.

"Is this . . . do you think . . . I mean . . ." I babble. My butt is suddenly glued to her passenger seat. Heck no am I getting out of this car.

"Jane!" Katie breathes. "Oh wow, Jane! Is this all for you?"

I look from one person to the next down the line of waiting customers. There are teenagers through senior citizens of all races and both genders standing in line, wearing their thick winter coats, scarves, and gloves. I try to say something, but my mouth is suddenly really, really dry.

"I . . ." I start, intending to tell Katie to take me right home, but I can't finish my sentence because I'm distracted by Katie's shocked expression.

Katie is still staring at the line. "There's got to be at least fifty people standing out here," she says. "It's like they are waiting for concert tickets or something."

I press my forehead against the window and stare. Suddenly I feel myself fall out of the car as Derek yanks the door open.

"Do you believe this? Do you believe this?" he says, excitedly pulling me out of the car like a mother lifting a toddler out of a car seat. Derek reaches in, grabs my backpack, and slings it over his shoulder. Katie yells something about going to find parking and pulls away from the curb.

Just then I spot the Channel 7 news van up on the curb and a reporter talking into his microphone. "What do coffee and love have in common?" he says. "Everything, if you ask these people lined up outside this local Wired Joe's."

"No, no," I moan. "Is this really just for me? I mean for Espressology night?"

Derek nods enthusiastically and puts his arm around me. He leads me away from the line and to the back entrance of the store, right next to the Dumpster. I can faintly hear the reporter interviewing a woman in line.

"This is freaking nuts, Derek. I can't do this!" I protest, shaking my head.

Derek pulls me into his office and helps me out of my jacket.

"Yes, you can, Jane. You are a pro at this. Look at all of the people who came to get matched. I've never seen anything like it!"

"Me neither," I say, slumping against his desk.

"Relax, Jane." He slips the red Espressologist apron over my neck. "Forget about the news. I told them you'd be too busy for an interview right now."

"An interview?" I squeak out. The closest I've ever gotten to television was when I was nine years old and the ABC weather anchor showed my crayon drawing of a rainy day that my mom had sent in. I glance down at my hands—they are red and shaking a bit.

"Ignore the line. Don't even think about it. Concentrate on one person at a time and remember how much fun you had last week." Derek starts to rub my hands in an effort to warm them up.

"You are freaking me out with all of this touching, Derek."

"Sorry, sorry," he says. "I'm just pumped."

I am relaxing slightly and actually feeling a bit of excitement in my belly. Either that or I am going to throw up all over the first person in line. But no, I can do this. I mean, I have done it. I'm going to march myself out there and I'm

going to make love happen for a lot of people. I'm going to
. . . but before I can complete this thought Derek pulls me out
of his office and pushes me right to the front of the store.
Right in the middle of my pep talk to myself.

"HOORAY!" A huge cheer breaks out in the store.

People are clapping and hooting and it is all for me. There
have got to be at least another thirty people standing in line
inside the store. Sarah, Daisy, Brenda, Frankie, and Em are
behind the counter ready to take orders and make drinks. And
even Seth, aka the Macchiato Maniac, is here, and he has
never worked a night shift before. He's a coffee master and
extremely fast and precise at making drinks. Em is looking at
me and shaking her head with an "I can't freakin' believe this"
look on her face. I give her my "I can't freakin' believe it
either" face.

"All right, all right, everyone," Derek's voice booms.
"Everyone calm down and we'll get started right away. Let's
let her through, people." He pushes into the crowd, making
me a path. I give my best homecoming-queen-riding-atop-a-
float wave. The clapping slowly dies down and I'm in a room
full of super-jazzed-up people. I take my seat behind my table
and set up my laptop and notes.

Deep breath.

"Okay, who's first?" I ask.

"I am."

A woman in a bright pink tracksuit with shiny silver
stripes pushes her way to the front of my table.

"Honey, I'm Darla. Darla Davenport from Oak Brook. You matched my very best friend in the whole world, Debbie Archer, last week, and she is so blissfully happy. You've got to pass some of your magic coffee love my way."

I can't help but laugh at this woman's enthusiasm.

"No problem," I say. "Give the barista behind the register your drink order and then we'll chat."

"I'd like a medium cinnamon mocha," she says to Em, snapping her gum in her mouth. She twirls around to face me. "You get that, hon? That's my favorite drink—a medium cinnamon mocha."

"Got it," I say as I type my notes into my spreadsheet. Ah, this is an old-timer. Cinnamon mochas, which are basically just mochas with added cinnamon syrup and cinnamon on top instead of whipped cream, have been off the menu for a long time now. I can see Daisy giving Em a questioning look out of the corner of my eye. I'm not worried though; the Macchiato Maniac will know how to make it. Darla pays Em and then places both hands onto my table.

"Okay, Darla, age and interesting tidbit?"

"Oh, I'm forty-five years *young*, baby doll. And my bowling average is 180. That's pretty interesting, isn't it?" She blows a bubble.

"Yeah, that's great."

Hey, if I don't match her, maybe I can hook her up on Em's ex-boyfriend's bowling league? I jot down the rest of Darla's data and tell her if I find a match I'll have him contact her soon. Darla takes her cinnamon mocha from Seth at the pick-up counter and leaves. I survey the line. "Next?" I call, and my jaw almost hits the table. "Ginny?"

"Yeah, I'm next," Ginny says. She slowly approaches the table.

I look around for Melissa, but I don't see her.

"You're here alone?" I ask, still surprised. I don't get why she's here. She and Melissa were just ragging on me earlier in the week about my Espressology.

Ginny nods.

"Hmm, okay," I say with hesitation, trying to figure out if this is going to turn into some nasty trick. "Go ahead and place your order at the counter and I'll begin entering your information." I look down at my sheet and mumble to myself, "Ginny Davis, small nonfat latte . . ."

"Um, no," Ginny interrupts.

"You're not Ginny Davis?" I prepare myself for whatever crap she's about to put me through.

"No, obviously my name is right. The drink is wrong."

"What? I've made you at least half a dozen small nonfat lattes myself."

"I know," Ginny replies with a sigh. "That's because it's Melissa's favorite drink."

"Oh." I suddenly feel sorry for Ginny. She can't even order what she wants to when she wants to. "What is your favorite drink, then?"

"I want a large mint mocha-chip frappycap, affogato style,"

Ginny says, and I'm absolutely floored at how completely polar opposite this drink is from what she usually orders. I glance at Em, who is ringing Ginny up, and I can see a look of appreciation on her face. Not a lot of customers know what *affogato* means—it's basically the frappycap with a shot of espresso floating on top.

"Sassy," I say, and Ginny giggles. You know, she's not half bad when Melissa isn't around. "I'm guessing you're eighteen?"

Ginny nods.

"Interesting tidbit about yourself?"

Ginny takes a moment to think. "Once a month I read my poetry at a poetry slam in a small café on the South Side."

"Really?!" I half ask, half yell. Who is this girl? Ginny smiles again. After I get the rest of her info, I tell her I'll have her match contact her once I find him.

"Thanks, and, Jane"—she points her index finger back and forth between me and herself—"we do have a doctor-patient confidentiality thing here, right?"

"Huh?" I give her a strange look.

"You won't tell anyone I was here, right?" she asks.

"No. Not if you don't want me to."

"I don't. Want you to, that is," she says.

"No problem."

Just then Daisy bellows out, "Large mint mocha-chip frappycap, affogato style."

"Well, that's me," Ginny says. "Have a good rest of the night."

"Thanks, you too," I say, still not sure how to take in the whole interaction.

◦◦◦◦

I've been working nonstop for three hours, meeting people, taking notes, and making matches as fast as I can. I've made five on-the-spot matches so far tonight, and I know there are a few more matches I can make once I have time to go through my notes. I'm exhausted. The line has finally dwindled. At least everyone fits in the store now, and no one has to wait outside. I'm stretching my arms up over my head when Derek comes up beside me at the table and whispers in my ear,

"Do me."

A sudden wave of nausea washes over me and I bring my arms down to my side at lightning speed.

"Excuse me?" I choke.

"Do me," he says again.

I look him in the eye. "Ever hear of a little thing called sexual harassment in the workplace, Derek?"

"No!" he yells, straightening and suddenly looking as horrified as I feel. "No, no, no!"

He leans down, puts his hand to the side of his mouth, and whispers, "I mean match me with someone."

His eyes dart left to right to make sure no one is listening.

"You want me to match you with someone? That is so cute."

"No, it isn't cute, and you better not tell anyone else about it. Just match me with someone and e-mail it to me. My favorite drink is a medium gingerbread soy latte."

"Awwwww," I say, surprised that a super-commercial Christmas drink is his fave. Derek glares at me and returns behind the counter to help take orders.

I help four more people: two slightly pudgy and balding brothers in their early thirties, a tall blond lesbian (my fourth lesbian of the night), and this beautiful super-leggy brunette catalog model. Now I'm face-to-face with a rather interesting character. Next in line is a girl with the blackest dyed Halloweenish-looking hair I've ever seen, a black zipper hoodie, a black T-shirt, and the most enormous pair of black baggy jeans (seriously, each leg looks like it could double as a skirt for me) covered in chains. She gives Sarah her drink order and then looks at me, expressionless.

"My name is Glinda," she says, glaring at me through eyes heavily coated in mascara and thick eyeliner.

"Like the good witch?" I ask. Whoops. Bad move.

"Yeah." She narrows her eyes and gives me a sarcastic smile.

"Sorry. Favorite drink?"

"Medium eggnog latte," she says. Oh puke, I hate eggnog, but whatever floats your boat, you know?

"Age?"

"Twenty-five." She looks exceedingly unhappy to be here.

"All right, Glinda, can you tell me some interesting tidbit about you? Just so I can get a better idea of who you are."

"Hmm." Her face softens while she thinks. "I'm a bad-ass singer. I even got to try out in front of the judges for *American Idol* when they came to Chicago."

"Omigod!" I squeal. "You met Simon, Paula, and Randy?!" I am a hard-core reality TV freak.

She nods. "But they never showed my audition on TV."

"Oh, bummer!" I say, typing her information into my laptop. Suddenly, I stop. Derek is off to the side grinding a one-pound bag of espresso for a customer. I look at Glinda, then at Derek, then at Glinda. Aha! Yes, yes, yes! Could she *be* any more perfect for him?

13

Katie, Ava, Em, and I are chilling over a late breakfast at Granny's Diner on Sunday.

"You should have seen it, Ava," Katie says. "I swear Jane almost crapped her pants when I let her out in front of the store."

"Nice image." I rub my eyes and tilt back in my chair. "Especially over breakfast."

Em nods. "It was *unreal*. I've never seen so many people in our store at one time."

"I couldn't believe it when I saw it on the news Friday night," Ava says. She stirs a Splenda into her green tea. "I kept watching to see if they were going to interview you, but they only showed you sitting at the table talking to customers."

I widen my eyes. "Oh, thank god they didn't. I was ready to toss my cookies just seeing all those people waiting for me. I could NOT do an interview on TV!"

"Can you imagine how ecstatic Derek must be?" Em says.

"Why?" I ask, concerned. Did Em somehow find out I had matched him? I e-mailed him yesterday morning with Gothy Glinda's info and he's probably contacted her by now. But I'm pretty sure he wouldn't have told anyone.

"Are you kidding? District must be throwing a parade for him with all the sales we pulled in Friday night. Heck, forget district, I bet the CEO of Wired Joe's himself called to congratulate Derek."

"You think?" I ask.

"Heck yeah," she says.

"It is pretty huge, Jane," Katie agrees. "A lot of the students over at St. Pat's have been talking about it."

"And the cast and crew at my community theater," Ava adds.

"The kids in my honor classes are talking about it, too," Em pipes in.

"*Shut up . . .*" I say. "No way are all these people talking about me. Are they? I'm going to totally freak out. I can't do this anymore. It's just getting way too big."

"Kind of late, Jane," Em says nonchalantly. "Derek is never going to let you out of it now. Besides, you only have two weeks left. You can do it."

"I don't think I can eat," I say, pushing my breakfast away.

"That's four ninety-nine you'll never see again." Katie laughs and the others join in. But I can't laugh right now. I'm feeling panicky again. I reach in my bag for a pack of Rolaids.

"Well, hey," Em says, interrupting my thoughts, "no one asked me about my date with Cam last night."

Please, not another installment of the Cam-Em love fest. Blech.

"How did it go?" Ava inquires. "Did he take you on a winter sleigh ride under the stars? Or just have an all-boys choir serenade you?"

Em smirks. "Nothing that romantic. Or cheesy. We just rented a Sandra Bullock movie and ordered a pizza at his house. But it *was* cozy," she adds.

"Snuggling on the couch is the best. Did he feel you up?" Katie asks.

Ew, ew, ew, I think, covering my ears. I don't want to hear this.

"I'll never tell," Em says, sipping her hot chocolate.

"Oh, he so did!" Katie grins. "You naughty girl!"

"Why am I naughty?" Em asks. "I didn't even say anything!"

"Exactly," Katie says, raising her eyebrows. Ava just laughs. I inwardly groan. Why am I even letting this bother me?

"Get this," Em tells us, "his *mom* was there."

"Eww," Katie and Ava groan.

"While you were on a date?" Katie asks. "Classy."

"I know, right?" Em sticks her finger into the whipped

cream on top of her drink and brings it to her mouth. "Anyway, she's kind of weird."

"How do you mean?" Ava asks.

"She just seemed really quiet and antisocial. She stayed in her bedroom all night."

"Maybe she wanted to give you guys some privacy?" I suggest.

"Sure. I guess," Em agrees. "But she looked pretty weird, too. She's real skinny. Like she's trying to be all Hollywood or something. Except she could stand a little makeup. Or some spray-on tan. And she's got this big poofy crazy-looking hair."

I can't believe what I'm hearing. Is Em really being this insensitive? What does she expect someone going through chemotherapy to look like? I mean, have some freakin' compassion.

"She's really demanding, too. She kept asking Cam to do things and get her stuff, you know? I kept thinking, get off your butt and get it yourself, lady. I felt really bad for him, even though he didn't seem to mind."

Oh . . . Em has no idea! Cam didn't tell her that his mom has cancer or that she's getting chemo and he's helping her. But why wouldn't he tell her something like that, especially since they are dating? He told me in the first five minutes that we talked.

"That does seem a little strange," Katie concludes. "Are you going to keep seeing him?"

"Oh, yeah," Em says. "I'm not going to let his mom bother me. Cam is fantastic. Isn't he fantastic, Jane?"

"Yeah, he's fantastic," I agree.

❧

I walk into work Sunday afternoon and Frankie and Sarah are behind the counter giving me massive smiles.

"Hey, guys. What's with the jack-o'-lantern smiles?" I don't have to wait long for my answer. Derek comes whooshing around the corner and gives me a big hug.

"Whoa," I say, pulling back. "What's the excitement?"

"You. You're the excitement! You are the best assistant manager in the whole world!" he exclaims. He must have hooked up with Glinda already. Only a girl would make him this excited. "You are wonderful, Jane!"

"Thanks, Derek, I like you, too."

"You just don't know how BIG this Espressology thing of yours has gotten. I mean it is HUGE!"

"Uh-oh," I say. "What now? Should I sit down?"

"Yes, definitely. Come with me so we can talk." Derek takes my hand and pulls me back to his office. I glance at Sarah, who is shaking her head and laughing softly.

A moment later the door is closed and we are looking at each other across Derek's desk. Derek takes a deep breath and pumps his fists up and down on the desk in excitement. "Brace yourself," he says.

133

"I already am." I look down at my white knuckles as I grip the armrests of my chair. "Just tell me."

"Okay, you know Friday was AMAZING, right?"

"Yeah . . ."

"I mean, sales were way through the roof." He puts one hand over his head to emphasize his point. "We took in ten times what we made the same Friday last year."

"Fantastic."

"Corporate has called a number of times," he tells me. "They think you are phenomenal. I'm sure we will both get huge holiday bonuses."

"Awesome!" I say with enthusiasm, already thinking about what I'll buy. A killer new outfit, and maybe I'll even splurge on a new handbag.

"Now here is the big news." Derek takes a deep breath, pushing out his chest. "Do you know that talk show *The Gabby Girlz*?" he asks.

"Oh, sure," I say. *The Gabby Girlz* is a show of three twenty-something women who sit around and talk about current events, interview celebs, host fashion segments, and so on. "I've seen it a few times. The girls always have on the cutest outfits."

"Excellent," Derek says. "Then you'll love what I'm going to say next. We're going to be a segment on their holiday show and they are coming here this Friday to film you doing your thing."

"No way!" I practically scream.

"Yes way," he replies. "They are doing a show on romance around the holidays and they want us to be on it."

"You've got to be kidding. I mean, this is really not that big a deal—"

"Oh, that's where you are wrong. This is a huge deal," he says.

"But we are just one Wired Joe's among a gazillion Wired Joe's."

"Yeah, but we are the only Wired Joe's with an Espressologist."

I sit back in my chair and stare at the stack of papers on Derek's desk, doing my best not to totally freak out and run home crying. "This is really going to happen?" I ask a few moments later.

"Mmm-hmm," he says. He looks thrilled.

"And there is nothing I can do to get out of it?"

"No, but don't worry. They just want to film you talking to some customers and then they'll ask you a few questions. It will be easy. And I'll be right there next to you the whole time."

"All right," I relent. Like I have any choice. "I guess there isn't really any way around it."

"It'll be great, Jane."

Yeah, right. As long as I don't throw up on a Gabby Girl. I've got to call Em and tell her ASAP.

14

"Wait a minute," Mom says. She stops in front of the huge toy store to turn and stare at me. School is out and both Mom and I have the afternoon off from work, so we are pretending to Christmas shop at Water Tower Place. We're really window shopping. The prices here are totally ridiculous. "You are going to be on TV?! On *The Gabby Girlz?*"

"Yup." Okay, I know it is totally bad of me to still not have told her or Dad about my being an Espressologist. And I probably still wouldn't tell her, but I kind of have no choice now—since I'm going to be on TV and all.

"I love that show. The girls always dress so cute," Mom says.

"I know," I agree. This is one of those moments when I know my mom is really my mom and not just some lady who found me on her doorstep and took me in (which I was

98 percent sure of up through freshman year in high school).

"I don't get the whole Espressology thing, though," she says. "What makes you an Espressologist?"

"Well, because I say so, mostly," I reply with a laugh, and we start walking again. "I'm the one who made it up. I'd been studying people and their drink orders for months and I just figured out a way to match them. And, well, it works."

"You've already been doing this for a couple of weeks, you say?"

"Yeah."

"Why didn't you tell Dad or me?" she asks.

Shoot. I knew she'd ask that. "I don't know," I say. "Partly because I didn't know how you'd react and partly because I didn't want you in there taking pictures or something and turning it into a scrapbook page."

"That's a fabulous idea!" Mom says.

"Oh no, Mom, don't do it."

"When you are putting yourself on television, you kind of leave me no choice. This is big!"

"I know. That's what scares me," I say. But she's not really listening anymore. I'm sure she's already envisioning what embellishments and stamps she will use on the scrapbook page.

"When does the show air? I'm going to have to call my mom, Grandpa Turner, all of your aunts and uncles . . ." Mom trails off and sits down on a bench, PDA now in hand, taking notes. I knew she'd react this way to the news. I guess this makes up for my not being a cheerleader freshman year like she wanted. I plunk down next to her on the bench and wait for her to stop writing.

"Mom?"

"Hmm?" She doesn't look up.

"Can we get going? Em is supposed to come by and help me get ready for Friday."

"One more second," she replies, and enters something else. "Okay, no problem, sweetie. Let's get you home." Mom loops her arm through mine and we head toward the exit. "I'm so excited that you are going to be on *The Gabby Girlz*, honey." She beams at me. I wish I was more excited.

༺੭ৎঌ༻

An hour later Em and I are plopped down on my bed, eating strawberry granola bars and staring at my Espressology notebook, lying open between us. Em is helping me memorize the different drinks and descriptions so that I can be even faster with my on-the-spot matches.

"Are you getting a lot of e-mail from your matches?" Em asks.

"Oh, loads! It's fun always having a ton of e-mail in my in-box. It's kind of like getting fan mail."

"Heck yeah, you have a ton of fans. Including me," Em gushes. "You are a real-life Cupid! How many matches have you made now?"

I quickly scan my totals in the spreadsheet. "Forty-six."

"That's amazing, Jane! Think about it . . . that's ninety-two people you've made happy for the holidays. No wonder you are getting fan mail!"

I smile. "I guess it really is pretty big. I didn't realize I had done so many matches already. Now I've got to match myself for the holidays."

"With Will?" Em teases.

"Of course!" I say. "He came in last night when I was working and I told him about Friday and *The Gabby Girlz* and everything. He said he wouldn't miss it for the world."

"Aww, he *so* likes you."

"I hope you're right. I mean, I think he does. He *is* giving me all the signals. When I was making his drink he stood at the pick-up counter talking to me and he even took one of the straws out of the holder and was rubbing it up and down my arm. I mean, who does that to someone he isn't interested in?"

"Um . . . riiiiiight," Em says.

"Oh, shut up," I tease. "It was cute. It was a cute thing, not a creepy thing."

"If you say so. Personally I like having my arm rubbed with plastic spoons, but, you know, whatever turns you on," Em says, dodging the pink-lips pillow I throw at her head.

"He was talking all seductively to me, too," I add.

"Really? What did he say?"

"Okay, the words weren't like über-seductive, but his tone of voice was. He was all deep and smooth and velvety. And he was telling me how he really needed a special someone in his life to share cold nights with—"

"Cheesy!" Em interjects.

"Whatever!" I return. "Anyway, like I was saying, he said he wants someone special and he was hoping that I would be able to find his perfect match on Friday night."

"So, you are really going to do it? You are going to match him with you?"

"Definitely," I say. "Enough with this flirting and teasing, I want to actually go on a date with Will. I'm going to tell him I'm his match. But after *The Gabby Girlz* thing is finished. I won't be able to think of anything else until the interview is over."

"Oh, Jane, I'm really happy for you. Really. I was feeling bad that I am all happy in love with Cam and you still don't have anyone."

My stomach drops a little. "Are you really in love with him now, Em?" I ask. "I mean *really*?"

"Well, I think so. I mean, it's not like Jason or anything. But nothing is going to be like Jason, right?"

"Is Cam in love with you?" I ask.

"I don't know," Em murmurs, thinking. "He's not that open with his feelings."

We are both silent for a moment. "Well, I'm happy for you, too, Em," I say, trying to look the part. Though I feel like crap for not actually being happy for my best friend.

15

I'm already getting anxious as I head into work today. Tomorrow is the big day. Tomorrow I will be on TV. Tomorrow I will meet the Gabby Girlz. I've been shopping all morning, looking for the right outfit. Okay, so I took one more tiny emergency day off from school. Just this one last time. I mean, I'm meeting the Gabby Girlz, who always look perfect, so I've got to look perfect, too. Not to mention I'm hooking up with Will tomorrow night as well. It's a HUGE night for me. I found *the* dress after three hours of shopping this morning. It's a clingy black (Derek insists that I still wear black under the red apron) V-neck dress with long sleeves that widen a bit at the wrists. It comes down to just above my knees, so I'm going to wear it with my new high-heeled suede black boots. I'm going to look *hot*. Em and I are going to get our hair and makeup done tomorrow afternoon, too.

I pull open the door of the café, ready for the familiar blast of holiday music and the smell of brewing coffee, but I'm stopped dead in my tracks. What the heck is this?

"Hey," Derek yells. "Come in and shut the door. You are letting all the cold air in." But I can't move. What happened to my Wired Joe's?

The place has been completely overhauled, or I should say it is still being completely overhauled. A crew of people I've never seen before are moving things around the store and adding various touches. The blue velvet chairs are gone and now there are several big velvety red loveseats with silver heart-shaped throw pillows. Every table is covered in a beautiful red tablecloth. The walls are covered with fabrics—all whites, silvers, and reds. Weird silver art pieces hang from the fabric. The blue, green, and white swirly covers of the lights hanging from the ceilings have been removed and replaced with red, white, and silver swirly covers. Beautiful antique-looking table lamps are set out everywhere, giving the whole store a more romantic lighting. Silver candelabras with red taper candles are set up on some of the shelves, and small canvases with quotes from famous love poems are spread throughout the store. All the tables have been removed from the north side of the store, and there is a big dark cherry-wood desk and a big Victorian-looking red velvet chair behind it. I run my finger along a large wooden sign lying on the desk, waiting to be hung. THE ESPRESSOLOGIST IS IN is artistically etched into the wood. Is this where I will be sitting?

"What do you think?" Derek asks, coming up next to me. "Is the sign all right? We are going to hang it up behind you."

"It . . . it's amazing," I finally say. It really does look beautiful. "I can't believe how different the place looks."

"It does look good," he agrees. "We needed a face-lift for the show. There are more touches we'll add tomorrow night. Things like rose petals on the table and such."

I stare around the room. I suddenly feel people's eyes on me. The customers, ALL the customers, are looking at me. "Why is everyone looking at me?" I whisper.

"Because they know about tomorrow and they know you are our Espressologist. You are a celebrity."

"This is so wild," I say. "I'm going to go put my stuff down and relieve Daisy. She's giving me a dirty look. Not that that's a new thing." I head toward the break room. I can feel everyone's eyes following me. It's hard having so many people stare at you! I'm going to have to run to the bathroom and make sure I don't have a booger hanging out of my nose or anything.

❦

I've been taking orders for about an hour or so now and I'm semi—getting used to people staring at me. I'd really rather they not stare, but it isn't nearly as jarring as it was for the first fifteen minutes or so. I suddenly feel a whoosh of happiness as I see my number-one former regular come through the door.

"Gavin! I'm so glad to see you. Where've you been? Did you give up coffee?" Gavin steps up to the register, leans over, and gives me a big smooch on the cheek.

"Hey, Jane."

"Ooh la la, what was the kiss for? Not that I'm complaining or anything."

"For finding me the love of my life," he says emphatically.

"Simone?" I ask.

"Yeah. She's wonderful, she's just . . . everything to me. We're totally in love."

"Oh, Gavin, I'm sooooo happy for you! Here, let me pay for your iced vanilla latte today. You know you were my first Espressology match, right?" I ask.

"No. I didn't even know you matched me until Simone told me how you hooked us up and Sarah explained the whole Espressology thing. I had to come in to see for myself."

"Yeah, where have you been? You used to come in every day. What happened?"

He looks at me sheepishly. "We've been going to the Wired Joe's near Simone's apartment."

I grin. "You two-timer!"

"I knew you were going to say that," he says, laughing.

"So, it's like that, huh? A girl comes along and it's bye-bye, barista? Typical." I shake my head.

"Aw, come on, don't be mad."

"I'll forgive you on one condition," I say.

"What's that?"

"Can you and Simone come in tomorrow night? The Gabby Girlz are going to be here interviewing me and since you guys were my first match, maybe they'll want to talk to you."

"Really? The Gabby Girlz? That's cool. Sure, I'll talk to Simone about it tonight."

"Great. Here's your iced vanilla latte," I say, passing him the drink. "See you tomorrow, hopefully."

"See you," he says, and heads out the door.

16

I swear I'm going to fall over right here and die of nervousness," I announce to the room. We are in the living room of my apartment doing last-minute beauty touches before leaving for the coffee shop. Everyone is coming to the Espressology night with me: Mom, Dad, Em (though she will be working), Katie, and Ava.

"Stop moving," Em says, breathing hot garlicky air in my face. Never a mint around when a girl needs one, is there? She's busily plucking at a few of my stray eyebrow hairs that seem to have appeared from nowhere. We're all dressed up (even Em bought a new outfit to go under her blue apron) and ready to go, but Em keeps finding things to fix on me. "You have to look perfect. You are the star of the show."

"Stop reminding me or I'll throw up on you right here and now, and you'll have to go home and change."

"Well, we don't want you doing that, so I won't mention it again," she says.

"Oh, honey," my dad says. "You look beautiful. I feel like I should be taking a picture of you and your prom date." He laughs.

"It does kind of feel like that," I agree.

"You do look stunning, Jane. I'm going to take a picture —everyone squeeze together and say 'Cappuccino!'" Mom says.

"Cappuccino!" we all yell. *Click.*

"Are we ready to roll?" Em asks.

"I guess it is now or never," I say, thinking *never* sounds fantastic about now. Dad heads out ahead of us to retrieve the car from the parking garage. We troop down to the street to wait for him to pull around. I'm clutching my bag with my notebook and laptop inside.

"Relax, Jane," Mom says, rubbing my hand. "You can do it." What a mom thing to say. How does she know that I can do it?

We pull up outside Wired Joe's and Dad lets us out. I suddenly feel like I should have rented a limo to bring me, since there is a long red carpet outside the store and it is sectioned off with red velvet ropes. There are, my god, what look like hundreds of people in line, watching me get out of the car. There is a big trailer parked right on the road, completely blocking traffic. It must be because of *The Gabby Girlz*. Suddenly there's a million flashes from cameras. It's like a fireworks show in front of my face. What is this, paparazzi? Do *I* have paparazzi? I mean, no doubt there is a celebrity some-where adopting a foreign baby that they should be taking pic-tures of, right? *I'm* not that interesting. But everywhere I look, people are taking pictures. People in line are holding up their cell phones in my direction and snapping shots. I stand there frozen with an undoubtedly stupid expression on my face, and I feel Em and Mom on either side of me lead me into the café.

The store is empty except for Derek, five baristas ready to work, and a lighting and camera crew setting up. No sign of the Gabby Girlz. Derek shut down the store for the last hour to set up for the show.

I look over at my beautiful desk. It's covered with candles and rose petals. It looks amazing. My sign is hanging off a gold nail on the wall behind my chair. There are candles and roses everywhere, and the smell of espresso is more intense than I ever remember it being before. It's like they're piping it in somehow. Derek steps up to me and helps me take off my jacket.

"You look fantastic, Jane," he tells me.

"You look great yourself." Derek is wearing a black suit with a deep red silk tie. I've never seen him this dressed up.

"Thanks," he says, and immediately gets back to business. "Here is what's going to happen. You go on and set yourself up at your desk. Then the Gabby Girlz are going to come in and briefly meet you, and their crew will adjust their lighting."

I nod, feeling my stomach tighten with nerves.

"They'll start out getting footage of you working with the customers for about half an hour to forty-five minutes. Then we'll take a break for them to conduct the interview with you." I nod again, afraid if I do open my mouth something gross will come flying out of it. "They'll ask you just a few questions. Two, three minutes, tops. And then that's it. It'll be a snap. Relax."

"A snap. Sure," I mumble. I move to my desk to have a closer look at the setup. Suddenly there is a roar of noise from the sidewalk and the store is lit up from the flashbulbs going crazy outside the windows. "What's going on?"

"It's them! It's the Gabby Girlz!" Em squeals, looking out the window.

"They're coming in," Mom says. My stomach flip-flops so hard that I fall back into my new red chair. The front door of the store flies open with a whoosh of cold air. The Gabby Girlz—Mackenzie Estrella, Hope Stewart, and Olivia Clark—stride in with an entourage of their people. Young girls, probably personal assistants, come in laden with big wardrobe bags, bottles of water, and BlackBerrys.

Derek rushes up to greet them. "Ladies, welcome. We are so happy to have you here at our store." The women barely register that he's there.

Olivia, whom I always considered the nicest of the three on the show, steps out front and extends her hand to Derek. "Nice to meet you," she says. "Cute place." She glances around the room, taking in the decor with a nod of appreciation.

"Thank you," Derek says. "Can I introduce you to our Espressologist?" He turns in my direction. "Jane, come here," he hisses.

I slowly pull myself out of the chair and walk toward the group. Holy lighting and makeup crew, these women are old! Wait a minute, isn't the whole premise of the show that they are a group of twentysomethings? They look that way on TV, but up close, well, these ladies have got to be well into their forties. Maybe even Mom's age. I feel duped. I seem to be the only one noticing, though, because the rest of the group is all buzzing with excitement.

"Ladies," Derek says, "I'd like you to meet Jane."

"Nice to meet you, Jane," Hope says as she peers at me over her Hollywood sunglasses and holds out one limp hand while the other presses a pink cell phone to her ear. I take it and give her hand a squeeze. I always find it a little creepy when people wear sunglasses at night. I just don't get it. Hope nods and walks past me to a corner table to finish her conversation.

"Jane, we've read the briefing about what you're doing here," Mackenzie says, grabbing my hand and shaking it firmly. "What a riot! Should make a good show."

A riot?

Olivia grins and offers her hand. I take it and try to look

enthused. "Don't be nervous, sweetie. Has someone briefed you on what is going to happen?"

I nod.

"Good," she says. "Then just get yourself situated and we'll get started."

"Okay," I mumble.

Em comes over, loops her arm through mine, and guides me back to my new desk and chair.

"Chill, Jane," she encourages me. "Just don't even think about it. Pretend it is a regular night."

"You're right. I can do this." I sit and look through my notes for what seems like the hundredth time. A few moments later Derek announces that he's opening the door and I brace myself. Here we go.

❧

The room quickly fills with people waiting to be matched, and some who are just here for support. Glinda is standing near Derek, looking proud to be with him. Gavin and Simone are here, arm in arm. Cam gives me a thumbs-up from behind a display of coffee mugs. And Will made it, too. He's about forty people back in line. I'm getting butterflies again. Tonight is the night I match Will, a five-shot espresso over ice, with me, a large iced nonfat mocha, no whip. Okay, okay, so it doesn't seem like a match right off, but I'm sure it will work. It has to.

I'm feeling better seeing some friendly faces. But then, ugh, Melissa. What is *she* doing here? She said she would never want me to match her. And so help me god, if she says anything nasty to me and it gets on camera . . .

Derek holds up his hands and speaks. "Welcome, everyone. I'm glad you all made it for our third Espressology night." There are whoops and hollers from the crowd, and some people clap. "Thanks," Derek continues. "As you know, tonight is very different, as *The Gabby Girlz* is here taping a segment." The crowd cheers again, even louder this time, and Mackenzie, Hope, and Olivia turn and give the crowd a wave from where they are doing last-minute prep in the corner of the store. "We are going to get started now. Try to ignore the cameras as best as you can. Just step up to the counter, place your order with one of our baristas, and then give Jane your information." The crowd cheers a third time when they hear my name. I can feel my cheeks redden a bit at all the attention.

I am poised at my desk with my fingers on my keyboard—ready to go. I can hear Hope talking to the camera at the other end of the store: "The Espressologist is in, at least at this local Chicago Wired Joe's." I'm going to have to block her out if I'm going to do this.

A timid-looking guy in his early twenties places his order with Em and then steps up to my desk. He has dark hair and light brown skin. He's wearing a long-sleeve plaid shirt tucked into khakis.

"How are you doing tonight?" I ask, smiling. He nods at

me and hands me a piece of paper with all of his details on it. Wow, he's prepared.

I type his info into my spreadsheet: Naushad Raheem, male, twenty-one, gamer.

"Whoops," I say, "I don't see the most important item. What's your favorite drink?"

Naushad smiles at me and shrugs. "I like small zebra mochas."

Well, dang. I didn't see that one coming. A zebra mocha is half regular mocha, half white chocolate mocha. I was about to peg him at something tamer, like a COD (coffee of the day). I type in *zebra mocha* and flip open my notebook to refresh my memory of this drink.

Small or Medium Zebra Mocha

Smart and spicy, this person likes to try unusual things and has an adventurous streak. Creative and witty and sure to be fun. Fair looks—not a rock star, but not a DMV Clerk. Her: Possibly a writer or artist and most likely has a good heart. Him: Most likely into computers, mainly communicates with the opposite sex online. Soft-spoken.

I can see this now, I think. Good thing I checked or I could have totally screwed up this guy's love life. "Naushad," I say, "I've got all of your information. If I find your match, I'll have her contact you." He nods and moves to the counter to wait for his drink.

I see Em hand the next guy in line his receipt and he turns to look at me. Hmm, he's pretty cute. Tall, at least six-one, a tiny bit overweight but broad-shouldered, with short dark buzz-cut hair. "Name?" I ask.

"My name is Rick," he says. "My favorite drink is a medium americano and I'm here in search of my angel." Aw, he's kind of sweet. I expect I'll be able to match him tonight. I flip through a few pages of my notebook to find the entry.

Medium Americano
Clueless but a patriot. He walked into Wired Joe's unprepared for what he came face-to-face with. A hundred different combinations swirled before his eyes: mocha, latte, cappuccino, espresso. The only word he even slightly recognized was American, so he ordered an americano. Wimp. And a medium at that! He was a middle child, second string on the h.s. football team—the Peter Brady of the coffee world.

Yikes! I must have been in a bit of a mood the day I wrote that. I'm not saying it is wrong, but I have to add an addendum. It's my book, so I can alter the description when I need to. I quickly scribble:

Addendum: Also may just prefer simplicity in life, straightforward guy's guy looking for love. Average across the board but a little romantic spark.

"So, Rick, tell me something interesting about yourself."

"I can speak five languages," he says.

"Impressive!"

"Yeah, I was a translator in the army for ten years."

"Cool. Stick around for a bit, Rick; I may be able to match you tonight."

"Great," he says with a satisfied expression, and heads to the counter to get his coffee.

I sneak a peek at the Gabby Girlz. They are all watching me and look thoroughly entertained. I continue to talk to customers for another half an hour or so and then Derek steps up to the desk.

"Jane, time for the interview," he says.

"Really?" I ask. He nods. I glance over at the Gabby Girlz, who are getting their makeup and hair checked.

I can do this.

17

The Gabby Girlz producer instructs me to hop up on my desk for the interview. I carefully cross my right leg over my left, trying for the cutest angle possible and the best opportunity at getting my boots in the shot. These babies were born to be on TV. The crew adjusts the lights and runs a last sound check. Will winks at me from his place in line. He is a few spots from the front and only moments away from finding the love of his life, aka me.

"All right, let's do this," Hope says, sitting next to me and smoothing down her skirt one last time. She faces the camera and puts on a hugely cheesy grin.

A director calls, "Ready for you in five, four, three, two . . ." He points to Hope.

"I now have the opportunity for a one-on-one with the

famous local Espressologist, Jane Turner," Hope says to the camera, and I smile. "So, Jane, tell me how you got started with all this." She whooshes her hand in a circle near her head.

"Well, it all started with a notebook."

"Really?" she asks needlessly.

"Yeah. You see, I've been observing people for a long time and I just kept a lot of notes on drinks and the type of people who ordered them." Hope, Mackenzie, and Olivia are all nodding their heads at me enthusiastically. It's making me feel kind of weird but I continue on anyway. "One day it occurred to me that one of our regulars, a medium iced vanilla latte, would be perfect with a customer who had come in for the first time, a medium dry cappuccino. I checked my notebook to review the personalities I've recorded for these drinks and I was right—they were a perfect match."

"You're kidding!" Mackenzie says.

"Um, no," I say. Duh. Would she be here interviewing me now if I was kidding?

"It obviously works," Olivia says, nodding at the line of people and saving Mackenzie from her stupid comment.

"Yeah, it does. The first couple I matched, Gavin and Simone, are actually here tonight."

"Fantastic! Where are you guys?" Mackenzie asks. Gavin raises a hand. Mackenzie heads over to talk to him and the cameras follow. Whew. I have a breather. I scoot around on the desk and grab my ice water. I take a quick drink and pat my forehead with a napkin. Man, it is hot with all these lights! A moment later Mackenzie is back by Hope's side and I quickly shove the water glass and napkin behind my back.

"It is so amazing that the matches work," Hope says. "You've really got something here."

I nod.

"So, after you matched a few of your friends, you decided to start matching the rest of the community?"

"Yeah, well, Derek—Derek Peters, he's the manager of our coffee shop—and I decided it would be a fun event for the month of December." One of the cameras zooms over to shoot Derek. "A finding-love-for-the-holidays kind of thing," I add.

"And your record is remarkable!" Olivia says with an encouraging smile. "How many people have you matched now?"

"Somewhere around fifty couples."

"That is so cool," Mackenzie says, and I find this a bit jarring. It is strange to hear someone as old as her saying, "That is so cool."

"It totally is," Hope agrees. "And next we are going to watch Jane make one of her famous on-the-spot matches and then follow them out on their first date."

"We are?" I practically scream at Hope. What the heck is this? I swerve on the desk to face Derek and look at him, my jaw dropped.

"Yes, we are," she tells the camera. "Right after this break."

The director yells, "We're clear!"

I look over at Em, who has been leaning on the pick-up counter watching the interview, and give her my "I'm screwed" face. She gives me back her "yup, you're screwed" face.

⸎

"What the heck, Derek?" I scream at him once we are safe behind his closed office door. As soon as the little red light on the camera went off I jumped down from the desk, grabbed Derek by the arm, and yanked him back to his office.

"What?" he says, like he doesn't know.

"How the heck am I supposed to just do an on-the-spot match now?"

"You've done plenty of them. I don't see what the big deal is."

"Are you kidding me? I don't know when they are going to happen. They just happen. I can't plan them!" He stares at me blankly. "You know that, Derek."

"Well, you are going to have to, Jane. Hope already announced that you were going to do it."

"But I can't!" I wail, plunking down in a chair and covering my face with my hands.

"You have a few minutes," he says. "Go over the people that you met tonight and see if you can match anyone."

"Yeah, because it is just that easy," I mutter sarcastically. I rub the bridge of my nose with my index fingers and run through the people that I met tonight. I told that Rick guy to stick around. Is there anyone here that I can match him with? What about that mountain-climber chick? Eh. No. There was that nice nurse. But she's in her mid-forties and Rick is in his mid-thirties. Not sure if that will work either. I'm going to freakin' KILL Derek.

An assistant producer pops his head into the office. "We're back in sixty seconds. We need you out here now." My mouth drops open for the second time in five minutes and I shoot Derek daggers.

"No," I insist in a low voice. "I can't do it."

"Come on, Jane," Derek coaxes, giving my arm a little pull.

"No," I say more defiantly. "You can't make me go out there. It'll be too embarrassing."

"Come on." He pulls me up from the chair and pushes me toward the door. I'm not moving my feet and he is actually sliding me out the door. Stupid slippery new boots.

Derek doesn't let go of me until I'm sitting on the desk again and a girl is touching up my makeup. Seriously, I have no idea what I am going to do. NO IDEA. I just can't do this. I turn to Hope. Maybe I can reason with her?

"Listen, I can't just *do* an on-the-spot match. It doesn't work like that. Besides, have you guys really thought it out? I mean, who is going to let you just follow them out the door and on a date? It won't work." I shake my head. There. I told her and it makes perfect sense. They'll have to make some sort of statement and we won't have to do this.

"I'll do it," a girl's voice says from the crowd of people.

"Who said that?" Hope asks.

"I did." Melissa steps out from the crowd and heads for my desk.

"What? You?" I spit at her. "But you said you'd never let me match you. You said it was stupid and you didn't need it and you could find your own dates."

"Yeah, well, I changed my mind," Melissa tells me smugly. She turns to the Gabby Girlz. "I'll sign whatever you want. You can follow me on a date."

"She's our girl!" Hope yells.

My jaw drops for the third time tonight. Seriously, my chest is gonna be bruised from my chin hitting it again and again like this. I look at Melissa and the Gabby Girlz. Why am I even here? They all have their minds made up and they don't seem to need me. Except for the matchmaking part.

I contemplate making a run for the door when the director announces, "We're back in five, four, three, two . . ."

18

The lights are burning on my face and I can feel sweat beading at my temple. Hope says something to the camera, has Melissa step up to the desk, and introduces her. Then they turn to face me.

"All right, Jane," Hope says. "Do your thing."

Okay. I have to think fast. I have to match Melissa with someone here. And it has to be someone compatible. It has to be a match that actually works or I'll look like a big fat fraud on national television. What am I going to do? I need to stall. I stand up and slowly walk behind the desk and take a seat in my chair.

"Melissa," I ask, slowly, "what is your favorite drink?" Like I don't already know.

"I simply *adore*"—Melissa smiles at the camera—"small nonfat lattes."

"Okay," I say. "Age?"

"Eighteen," she answers with a giggle. "Like you didn't know." I sigh heavily as I type the information in, trying to figure out what I'm going to do.

"Interesting tidbit?" Darn! My voice quivered.

"Since you asked," Melissa says, perching on my desk now and facing the camera instead of me, "I'm going to become a famous fashion designer. I'm studying at the renowned School of the Art Institute of Chicago and I've already designed these fab sparkly leg warmers PERFECT for the current leggings trend." She kicks her legs out for the camera to see. "And you can get them at www—"

"We'll cut you off there," Olivia interrupts, giving Melissa a dirty look. Ah. So that was her deal. She's trying to sell some lame-o leg warmers. What is she thinking? Leg warmers need to stay dead and buried in the eighties. "Jane," Olivia continues, "do you have a match for Melissa?"

"Give me just a minute," I say, trying to look calm. I check the list of people I met tonight. Ugh. No one seems right for Melissa. I can maybe, possibly send her with the veterinarian but a) he's too old and b) he's too smart for her. I don't know what I am going to do.

"Ready, Jane?" Hope asks. "We are on television, you know." All the Gabby Girlz laugh. Tee hee hee. This is SO not funny, people.

"Um . . ." I scan the crowd hoping for the perfect match to just fall from the sky and into the wooden barrel of stuffed holiday bears. And then it hits me. A match. It *would* work. But no. I couldn't. No, no, no. I just can't. Not him. Not with her.

"Jane?" Hope prompts again, eyes wide and giving me a "hurry up" look.

"Okay . . ." I start, "the perfect . . . um . . . match for uh . . . a small nonfat latte is a . . ." I take a deep breath and close my eyes. "A five-shot espresso over ice."

"Ooh," Mackenzie says, like she just heard the most scandalous thing ever. "And who is that?"

I can literally feel my heart breaking into a million pieces.

"Will," I whisper, and point in his direction.

❧

I can feel the tears stinging my eyes as Will and Melissa exchange introductions and prepare to head out for their date. Hope, Mackenzie, and Gabby thank me and say a few more words, but I don't really hear them. Suddenly, the lights flip off me and the cameras move. Some guys with handhelds follow Melissa and Will out the door for their date. I stand up, turn, and run out of the store.

I run and run, tears streaming down my face, for what seems like miles but is really only a few blocks. What did I do? What did I just do? How could I give over my Will to that . . . that evil witch? And what was with the way they looked at each other? All pleased and stuff. Ugh, it made me want to puke all over them. That would have been fun TV. I run another block and then turn around the corner so no one from the store can see me on the sidewalk.

I lean against the brick wall of a tall high-rise, breathing heavily. I really need to work out more. I slouch down to a squat against the building, pulling my dress over my legs. It's cold out and I didn't stop to grab my jacket when I sprinted away from the store.

I lay my head back against the building and look up. I'm just under the El train track. I love the El. I've loved the El ever since I was a little girl. Whenever my mom and I or my dad and I were out running errands and we came near the El track, I would beg them to let me stand there for a few minutes and watch the trains zoom by overhead. There was always a train rushing by every few minutes. Lights would flash, the track would shake, and the train would make a clattering rumble as it passed. I used to think the track would break and the train would crash right in front of me and I would leap out of the way just in time. Maybe that will happen now, only I won't be able to leap fast enough and I won't have to go back to the store. Then I won't have to see Melissa and Will . . . together. I close my eyes and listen as a train goes racing past overhead.

"Hey," a male says, and I jump two feet into the air.

"I have Mace!" I scream, bracing myself for a confrontation with a mugger.

"Good. You should always be safe when you are walking alone at night," Cam says in a calm voice.

"Oh, my god, Cam, you scared the crap out of me. And I don't really have Mace."

"Whew." He fake wipes his brow. "What happened back there?"

I pull my arms tightly around me, shivering from the cold. "Nothing."

"It didn't look like nothing," Cam says. "Everyone is wondering where you went."

"I can't go back." I shake my head as a fresh tear rolls slowly down my right cheek.

"Jane," Cam murmurs, "you can tell me. What's wrong?" He puts his right arm around me and I can feel myself weakening.

"It's just . . . you know I hate Melissa, right?"

"Yeah, I remember she was really evil to you that day we were studying."

"Well, Will was supposed to be, I mean, I was going to match Will——" I start to cry harder.

"Don't cry, Jane." Cam pushes my hair, wet with tears, away from my face.

We are standing really close to each other. I cry for a few more seconds.

"What about Will?" Cam asks when I'm down to a sniffle.

"I was going to match Will with me tonight," I say finally.

"With you?" Cam looks shocked. I nod. "But why?"

I look down at the ground and mumble, "Because he's perfect."

"Perfect for you?" Cam asks. "Are you sure?"

"Pretty sure," I say, and another tear escapes. We're both silent for a few minutes. Another train goes thundering by overhead. My lips are shivering hard now and my arms are shaking. Cam slips off his jacket, wraps it around me, and turns me toward him.

"I know that right now it doesn't seem like it," he says, "but Will is not the perfect guy for you."

"Yes, he is," I argue.

"No, he's not," he retorts.

"Well, if you know so much"—I look him straight in the eye—"then who is?" Suddenly, before I can even comprehend it, Cam is kissing me. He has both hands behind my neck, fingers in my hair, and he is giving me a warm, slow, gingery-tasting kiss. And it is good. I mean REALLY good. I don't think I've ever been kissed like this. My toes feel warm, and not just from the run in high-heeled boots. And though I thought I'd be kissing Will and not Cam tonight, I close my eyes and just enjoy the kiss for however long it is going to last.

A few moments later Cam pulls back and my lips get cold again. He still has his hands behind my neck, but I can sense that he has pulled a few inches away. I open my eyes and stare at him, not sure what to say next. He apparently doesn't know what to say either. Well, one of us has to talk.

"Cam, I—" I begin, and then stop, stiffening as my body is filled with horror. I'm staring over Cam's right shoulder.

"What? What's wrong?" he says with concern. He slowly turns to see what, or in this case whom, I'm looking at.

Em.

Cam's hands drop from my neck like I'm on fire and we both stare at her. Em is standing maybe twenty or thirty feet away, holding my jacket. She stands there for another second or two and then throws my jacket on the ground and runs back in the direction of the store.

"I have to go after her," I tell Cam.

"No, let me," he says.

"No, she's my best friend. I have to do it." I run in the same direction as Em.

19

I was never one for school sports, but experience on the cross-country team would really come in handy about now. I can't find Em anywhere. Did she slip behind a building? Did she duck into one of the stores? Did she turn down a different block? I don't know how she got away from me, but she did. I've looked down each block on the way back to Wired Joe's, and nothing. I'll have to peek in and see if she is there. I doubt she'll stay at work tonight, but she does have to get her things. I don't want to go back to work; I don't want to face all those people again tonight, but what choice do I have? I have to find Em.

At Wired Joe's, I peek through the glass, looking for any sign of Em. I am instantly relieved to see that the Gabby Girlz and their crew have packed up and left. I feel a little pang of guilt at the line of people still waiting for me to come back and match them. Yikes.

Brenda, Sarah, and the Macchiato Maniac are working behind the counter. Mom and Dad are sitting on a cushy red velvet loveseat drinking cappuccinos. And Katie is standing near the condiment bar, flicking sugar packets against her thumb. I don't see Ava. Maybe she's in back consoling Em. I tap at the glass, trying to get Katie's attention so I can ask her if she's seen Em.

Tap tap tap. Tap tap tap.

"Jane!" Derek booms from behind me.

"Ahhh!" I jump a foot off the ground. "Derek, why are you always sneaking up on me?"

"What are you doing outside? Right in the middle of an Espressology night?" he yells, both hands on his hips. He totally looks like my mom when she's pissed at me.

"I . . . I needed some air," I say.

"You couldn't wait five minutes to get some air? You couldn't wait until they wrapped up the *Gabby Girlz* interview first?"

"Yeah. I really needed it."

"Well, if you are done getting your *air*, you need to get right back inside and finish helping that long line of people. You left us all waiting on you, Jane."

"Wait," I say. "Have you seen Em? I have to find Em first."

"No, she took off, too. What is with you girls tonight?

Why is everyone taking off when they are supposed to be working?"

"Derek, I have to go after her," I say, giving him a pleading look. "You don't understand, I really, really have to find her."

"And you can. After ten, when you are done working. Right now you have to get back in there and matchmake."

"But, Derek—"

"No. There is nothing you can say. Now get in there."

Everyone claps and cheers for me again, but this time I can't even muster up a smile. All I can think about is Em and how much she must hate me right now.

❧

On Wednesday afternoon, I'm lying on the couch in my living room watching *Dr. Phil*. He's yelling at some chubby woman in an ill-fitting light green suit, telling her in his heavy Texan accent, "When you choose the behavior, you choose the consequences." He might as well be talking to me. I chose the behavior (well, really Cam did, when he kissed me, but I didn't exactly push him off me or anything) and now I have to live with the consequences of Em never talking to me again and losing my very best friend in the whole world.

I don't know how I got through the rest of Friday night. I know I talked to people and got down their information for future matches, but I didn't do any more on-the-spot matches that night—much to the disappointment of that cute army

guy who stuck around until closing. I just couldn't stop thinking about Em. And I tried calling her over and over again
every chance I got, but she wouldn't pick up my calls. I've tried
texting her, IMing her . . . heck, I even went to her apartment
on Sunday to try to talk to her, but her mom said Em was too
sick to have company. I've felt so terrible ever since she saw
Cam and me kissing. I called in sick to work on Sunday and
Tuesday. I haven't been able to eat a thing either. Except for
Ben & Jerry's cookie dough ice cream. Two pints since Friday.
I feel just wretched. And now Dr. Phil is yelling at me
through the television.

Cam has been calling me, too. Twice anyway. I told my
mom to take messages, though. What am I supposed to say to
him at this point? And that kiss! That totally great kiss—
what did it mean? He can't like me and I can't like him, right?
He's with Em. How way way wrong would that be for me to
hook up with her boyfriend? Of course that is what she
thinks right now, but if she would let me I would totally
explain that it was just a . . . a . . . I don't know what it was.
Argh!

"Honey." Mom interrupts my thoughts and pushes my
legs over so she can sit down on the couch. "You can't live on
the couch watching silly talk shows the rest of your life."

"It's not silly, it's educational, and yes I can," I say without
taking my eyes off the television screen.

"Em still won't talk to you?" Mom asks gently.

"No."

"Don't worry, sweetie," she says, patting my leg. "She can't stay mad at you forever. You've been best friends for too long."

"Mmm-hmm," I mumble. I hope Mom is right. What would I do without Em? We sit there silently for a few minutes watching Dr. Phil rip into some other chick. Seems this one only likes to date married men. Like that is just some kind of coincidence. Get off my back, Phil!

"Your segment on *The Gabby Girlz* airs tomorrow morning at nine, you know. Are you going to watch it?" Mom asks.

"I don't know," I say, sitting up. And I really don't. On the one hand I want to see how I look on TV and how the interview came off, but on the other hand it'll be like death watching Will and Melissa on their date. "I don't know if I can."

"How about I record it and then you can decide if you want to watch it later?" Mom stands, and I nod my head in agreement and sink back into the couch.

I already know that Will and Melissa really hit it off on their date. Daisy was only too eager to tell me everything she knew when I called in sick on Sunday. She said that the assistant producer of *The Gabby Girlz* had called Derek and told him that the segment was perfect. They were impressed with my matchmaking ability and how it actually worked. They said Will and Melissa were holding hands, kissing, and exchanging phone numbers before the end of the date. Real nice. I've been working on landing him for months and in just a few hours he's kissing her and giving her his phone number (and probably the *real* one at that). Fat chance he'll ever get free drinks from me again. I'm so done with guys. Maybe I'll get a goldfish.

The phone rings.

"Honey," Mom calls, "can you get it?"

"Can you?" I ask, not wanting to move any more than I have to.

"No, just pick it up, Jane. Maybe it's Em?"

"Fine!" I'm mad that I have to get up and walk all the way across the room to where the phone is parked upright in its charger base. I press TALK and put the phone up to my ear. "Hello?"

"Jane?" a male asks.

"Yeah, this is," I say with a sigh.

"It's Derek. How are you feeling?"

"Oh, you know. So-so."

"I've been worried about you. Think you'll be in tomorrow?"

"Probably not. I still have a bit of a fever."

"Well, Friday is our last Espressology night. You have to make it in for that at least," he tells me.

"Oh, yeah," I reply. "I almost forgot about it."

"It's just one more week. You can do it, Jane," he says encouragingly. "You've done a fantastic job. I'm sure you'll get something out of all this—that big bonus or something." I guess if I can't have a boyfriend, a bonus isn't so bad.

I sigh again. "I'll be there."

I glance over at the calendar on the wall. I can't believe how fast the month has gone by. It's almost Christmas. All these people I've matched will have boyfriends and girlfriends to cuddle with in front of fireplaces with cups of cocoa for the holidays. Even that nasty stupid Melissa. And what do I have to cuddle? A possible bonus. Yay.

20

I get to work an hour before Espressology night starts on Friday, ready to put on my happy face, make some love connections, and wrap up my Espressology career. The glitz and glam from the television taping is gone now, and it's back to my same old Wired Joe's. Em's working behind the counter and I totally want to run over and give her a big hug, but she won't even look at me. How am I going to get through this?

I slink past Em to put away my purse and coat. I take a sideways glance in the mirror at tonight's outfit and am pleased that I still look good despite my incredibly icky mood. I picked a pair of black leggings, ballet slippers, and a really cute long black off-the-shoulder sweater tonight, envisioning how good the red straps of my Espressologist apron would look on my bare shoulders. I'm really going to miss being able to wear the variety of cute clothes on Friday nights once I have to go back to my Wired Joe's uniform.

I should go help at the register for a few minutes, but I have to figure out what I'm going to say to Em. She can't really ignore me the entire night, can she? I sit down at one of the metal chairs in the break room, fold my arms on the table, and rest my forehead on my forearms. A moment later I see a pair of black Converse appear under the table. Em's shoes! I jolt up.

"Em!" Em is standing next to me, staring at me expressionlessly, her arms crossed. "Em, please don't be mad at me. Please—I would never do anything to hurt you, I swear!" She says nothing but continues to look at me. "I'm really, really sorry," I say in a much smaller voice, tears forming in the corner of my eyes. The room is eerily quiet and we stare at each other for what seems like forever.

"I know." She plops into the metal chair next to me. She sighs heavily and puts her legs up on a chair to her left.

"Are you still mad at me?"

She looks thoughtful, like she is really considering it. Finally she says, "No. I can't stay mad at you. You're my best friend. And it wasn't really your fault anyway."

"It wasn't?" I ask, totally shocked. "I mean, it wasn't, I don't think."

"I talked to Cam yesterday." Em turns to look me in the eye now.

"You did? What did he say?"

"I was pretty pissed at him, too. I wouldn't talk to him all week. But then yesterday I picked up the phone when he called and asked if we could get coffee and talk. And I said fine. We met at Capulet Coffee."

"Oh, Em, you really must have been upset. Capulet tastes like a mixture of raspberries and cat pee."

She smirks. "Coffee snob," she says.

"So what happened?"

"Well, apparently we were on two different pages with this relationship. I thought we were together—like boyfriend and girlfriend. He thought we were just friends hanging out."

"Huh? How did that happen?" I ask, thinking back to the various times she told me they were "in love."

"He maintains that he has always told me we were just friends. And I have to admit, he did say things like that. Like, when he'd introduce me to someone he'd say, 'This is my friend Em' or whatever."

"No way!"

"I thought he was trying to keep things interesting. You know—keep me on my toes or something," she adds.

"Wow."

"Yeah, wow," Em says. "And I thought about it a lot last night and today. I think maybe I was wanting to be in a relationship so I kind of put myself into one. Real or not. I was with Jason for so long that I didn't know how to do the Em-on-her-own thing."

"Oh, Em, I'm sorry it didn't work out."

"It's all right. I mean, I'll be all right. I had a really long time to think about it this past week. And Cam is cool and a lot of fun. Don't get me wrong—I think he's a great guy. But I don't think I actually was in love with him or anything."

"So why didn't you take any of my calls? Why did you ignore me? I've been miserable," I whine.

"Hey, I was pretty bloody pissed at you most of the week. I only came to this revelation yesterday after talking to Cam," she tells me.

"I had my phone on all day today," I mumble under my breath.

"Um, sitting next to you and can totally hear you."

"Seriously! Why didn't you call me and tell me this earlier?"

"I was letting you squirm a bit more. I mean, I am your best friend and you *were* kissing the man you thought I loved. That is *so* wrong," Em says.

"Yeah," I agree, slumping against the back of my chair. "I'm a sucky friend. He did kiss me, though. But I should have stopped him." Although it was a freaking fantastic kiss. We both sit for a few moments thinking.

"We're still best friends, right?" I ask at last.

"Of course," she says, reaching over to give me a hug. "Now your turn. I've been DYING to ask you all week—why the heck did you match Melissa with Will?!"

"I know, I know!" I exclaim, covering my face with both my

hands. "It was so stupid! But I didn't know what to do! Those Gabby Girlz put me on the spot. It was the only match I could see possibly working . . ." I trail off.

"But Melissa!" Em says. "You hate her."

"True," I agree.

"And not to ruin your night or anything, but they totally hit it off. Will was in last night and told me he was on his way to pick Melissa up for a date. He really likes her."

"I've heard," I say. "Big jerk. They can have each other. I hope I never see either of them ever again."

Just then Derek pops his head into the room. "Customers, ladies," he says.

I glance at my watch. Whoops—it's almost six. Time to go start the last Espressology night. I tell Em I'll see her in a few minutes and step in front of the mirror for last-minute adjustments.

❧

"Ladies and gentlemen," Derek booms loudly to the huge line of people wound around the store and out the front door. "Last chance to find a little love with your latte. Here she is one more time, our Espressologist, Jane!"

Everyone cheers and whoops and I feel a rush of excitement go through me again. Everything is going to be fine. I don't have Will, but at least I have my best friend back. And I'm different, stronger. I'm not the same weak, timid Jane I was before this whole thing started. My Espressology didn't just change all these people's lives, it changed me. And I have to say that this whole adoration thing is kind of addictive. I totally know how Oprah feels. I give the crowd a huge smile and head for my small table near the cash register. I stop dead in my tracks when I see who is first in line waiting for me. Melissa.

"What do you want?" I say, slipping into my seat and bracing myself for whatever crap Melissa is about to sling my way. "Didn't your match work out for you?"

"It did!" she exclaims. "It really really did. That's why I'm here. To thank you." Melissa is positively beaming. She actually looks altogether different. She's like blissful or something.

"Really?" I ask, trying to hold back a bit in case she is setting me up for some kind of insult.

"You really know what you are doing, Jane," she gushes. "I mean, I didn't believe it at first, but then you matched Will and me and he is just perfect! I'm so happy."

"I'm glad?"

"I have to do something to thank you."

"Don't worry about it," I say.

"No, I want to."

"Well," I say, thinking, "how about you just stop being snarky when you come in for your coffee?"

"Of course! That's easy. But I want to do something bigger for you."

"Really, I don't need anything."

"Wait, hear me out," she says. "I already know what I want to do for you."

"Okay . . ."

"You know how I attend the School of the Art Institute of Chicago? A little birdie told me that you want to go there, too, and you are saving up for the tuition. It's totally expensive."

"Yeah," I say, wondering where this conversation is going.

"Well, I can help you."

I shake my head. "No, you can't." What? Is she going to offer to pay my tuition with some secret stash of money? I should have known she was trying to mess with me.

"No, I can!" she insists. "My dad is in financial aid there. He helped me become independent of him and my mom so I could get loads of financial aid. How do you think I pay for school?" Interesting.

"Are you serious?" I ask, trying not to get my hopes up too much.

"Totally! I'll talk to him this weekend. I'm sure he will help you do the same."

"Wow. Well, thanks."

"No, thank you, Jane. And I'm sorry I've been such a witch to you in the past." I nod and we look at each other for another moment. "Can I get a small nonfat latte now?" she asks. I laugh and give her order to Em.

❧

It's nine-thirty and the final Espressology night is coming to an end. Ginny and Zane, the hot bass player I matched her with, stopped in for drinks half an hour ago. They both looked insanely happy. There are a few more people waiting in line and I have a free moment while Em and Sarah deal with a frap rush (half a dozen or so young teens who order frappy-caps). I scan my spreadsheet, searching for a match for the über-hunky doctor in his late twenties who ordered a mocha valencia—a mocha with orange syrup, an extra shot of espresso, whipped cream, and orange-colored sprinkles on top. It tastes just like those chocolate orange slices you can buy during the holidays at specialty grocery stores. I hear a rumbling in my line and I look up to see what is going on.

Cam. Cam is standing right here in front of my table smiling down at me.

"Hi," I say.

"Hi," he returns. Okay, this is a little awkward. Silence. Is he going to talk or what?

"Um, are you looking to be matched tonight?" I ask.

"Yep," he says with an even bigger smile. Okay, this is just plain weird now.

Fine. I'll play your game. I enter his name into my spreadsheet. "Age?"

"Nineteen," he replies.

"Favorite coffee drink?"

"Medium toffee nut latte."

"And what, pray tell, interesting tidbit can you give me

183

about yourself?" I raise one eyebrow at him, anticipating his answer.

"Well," he says with a smirk, "I TOO have the ability to match people based on their favorite coffee drink."

"Yeah right," I say, thinking he's teasing me.

"I can!" he insists.

"Then what do you need me for? You should be able to figure out what goes with a medium toffee nut latte all by yourself."

"I can," he says again.

"Well?" I ask.

"A medium toffee nut latte goes PERFECTLY with a large iced nonfat mocha, no whip," he answers, looking awfully proud and smug.

"Huh?" I say, momentarily confused. I quickly flip through my notebook and then it hits me—that's my favorite drink. I look back up at him. "It doesn't really, you know," I start, not able to stop the smile from spreading across my face.

"Jane," he says, taking my hands and pulling me up from my seat, "it does. Trust me." And then he kisses me. Right there in front of the customers, the baristas, and Derek. I feel the force of his warm lips press against mine and I don't want him to move. I want to stay right here kissing Cam forever. I can hear customers whistling and clapping, but I don't pull away from Cam. It's finally my turn—I found my match. Or really, he found me.

Acknowledgments

With many, many thanks to: My fabulous agent, Jenoyne Adams, for her never-ending energy, time, and dedication to all my books; my incredible editor, Janine O'Malley, for loving this novel and the main character, Jane, as much as I do; the rest of the FSG team (Jill Davis, Irene Metaxatos, John Nora, Karla Reganold, and Nancy Seitz) for their awesomeness; Deena Lipomi and Emily Marshall, for their endless support, cheerleading, and friendship; all of my critique partners, Deena, Emily, Julie, and Mandy, for always having amazing insights and suggestions; the supercool baristas at my local Starbucks, for letting me write the entire book from the same table in their store and letting me study them without thinking I was a freak; my mom, dad, brothers, and the rest of my great family for their continuous love and support; my four fantastic kids, Teegan, Maya, London, and Gavin, for making my every day sweet and fun and not holding it against me when I hit the cafés to write at night; and, most important, my wonderful husband, Athens, who always believed I could and would do this.

What's Your Drink of Choice?

Here are some recipes for you to learn to make coffee drinks just like the baristas at Wired Joe's. Enjoy!

JANE'S NONFAT ICED NO WHIP MOCHA

INGREDIENTS
Chocolate syrup
Skim milk
2 oz. espresso (double shot)
Ice

DIRECTIONS
Squeeze a decent amount of chocolate syrup into the bottom of a tall glass. Use your judgment, but 4 or 5 swirls are good. Fill the glass with skim milk.
Make a double shot of espresso. For fresher espresso, grind the espresso beans just before use. Pour the espresso into the glass of milk. Stir.
Add ice.

MELISSA'S NONFAT LATTE

INGREDIENTS
1 c. skim milk
2 oz. espresso (double shot)

DIRECTIONS
Steam the milk in a steaming pitcher. Point the steam wand toward the bottom of the pitcher to steam. Raise the tip of the wand to just below the surface of the milk to create foam at the surface. Pour the steamed milk into a mug, holding back the foam.
Make two shots of espresso. Pour the shots of espresso into the milk. Stir.
With a spoon, scoop leftover foam out of the steaming pitcher and place on top of the drink.

CAM'S TOFFEE NUT LATTE

INGREDIENTS Toffee nut syrup
1 c. 2% (or whole) milk
2 oz. espresso (double shot)
Whipped cream
Caramel sauce
Toffee

DIRECTIONS Pour 1 to 2 ounces of toffee nut syrup into a mug.
Steam the milk in a steaming pitcher. Pour the steamed milk into a mug.
Make a double shot of espresso. Pour the espresso into the milk. Stir.
Garnish with whipped cream, caramel sauce, and toffee bits.

DEREK'S GINGERBREAD SOY LATTE

INGREDIENTS Gingerbread syrup
1 c. soy milk
2 oz. espresso (double shot)
Whipped cream
Nutmeg

DIRECTIONS Pour 1 to 2 ounces of gingerbread syrup into a mug.
Steam the soy milk in a steaming pitcher. Pour the steamed milk into a mug.
Make a double shot of espresso. Pour the espresso into the milk. Stir.
Garnish with whipped cream and nutmeg.

EM'S COFFEE HOT CHOCOLATE

INGREDIENTS Chocolate syrup (or your favorite hot chocolate mix)
½ c. milk
½ c. brewed coffee
Whipped cream

DIRECTIONS Pour 1 to 2 ounces of chocolate syrup into a mug.
Steam your choice of milk in a steaming pitcher. Pour the steamed milk into a mug.
Fill it the rest of the way with your choice of brewed coffee. Stir.
Garnish with whipped cream.

GOFISH

KRISTINA SPRINGER

What did you want to be when you grew up?
Rock Star. Stage name: Tina Rockafina.

When did you realize you wanted to be a writer?
Fiction writer: only about six years ago. Freelance writer/ writing instructor: Sophomore year in college.

What's your first childhood memory?
Swimming in the baby pool in the backyard when I was about two.

What's your favorite childhood memory?
Christmas mornings—I can't really pick one.

As a young person, who did you look up to most?
My mom

What was your worst subject in school?
Math

What was your best subject in school?
English

What was your first job?
Day Camp Assistant Teacher when I was thirteen

How did you celebrate publishing your first book?
It released on my birthday, so it was an all-day celebration: spa day, stopping into a book store to sign copies, dinner out, and cake and presents for my birthday.

Where do you write your books?
In coffee shops—mostly Starbucks and Caribou.

Where do you find inspiration for your writing?
Everywhere! Though lots of ideas come from when I think about my own teen years.

Which of your characters is most like you?
Jane in *The Espressologist*

When you finish a book, who reads it first?
Deena Lipomi, one of my super cool critique partners

Are you a morning person or a night owl?
Morning

What's your idea of the best meal ever?
Pizza and cookie dough ice cream. Or just the cookie dough works too!

Which do you like better: cats or dogs?
Dogs

What do you value most in your friends?
Trust

Where do you go for peace and quiet?
Coffee shops

What makes you laugh out loud?
My four kids—they're hysterical!

What's your favorite song?
Carole King—"Anyone At All"

Who is your favorite fictional character?
Becky Bloomwood (from the Shopaholic series by Sophie Kinsella)

What are you most afraid of?
Something bad happening to anyone in my family

What time of year do you like best?
Fall

What's your favorite TV show?
Real Housewives of anywhere. I love them all. Okay, if I had to pick one: New York.

If you were stranded on a desert island, who would you want for company?
Just one? Okay, my husband. But I'd miss the kids!

If you could travel in time, where would you go?
Back to the Renaissance era. But I'd definitely need a castle with air-conditioning.

What's the best advice you have ever received about writing?
Don't quit.

SQUARE FISH

What do you want readers to remember about your books?
That they're fun!

What would you do if you ever stopped writing?
Audition for *Real Housewives of Chicago*

What do you like best about yourself?
I think I'm hysterical. At least I'm always entertained!

What is your worst habit?
Facebook

What do you consider to be your greatest accomplishment?
My four kids

Where in the world do you feel most at home?
Chicagoland area

What do you wish you could do better?
My makeup. And my hair. Maybe I'll go to beauty school if the writing and *Real Housewives of Chicago* thing falls through.

What would your readers be most surprised to learn about you?
That I'm addicted to spin classes. I LOVE them!

Tori is so sick of hearing about Sienna's new boyfriend that she makes up her own boyfriend to talk about. But what's she going to do when it's time to bring him to the school dance?

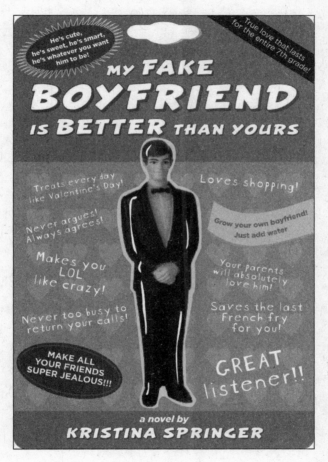

Find out what happens in

MY FAKE BOYFRIEND IS BETTER THAN YOURS

1

We're outta here in ten, Tor!" Mom screams from the bathroom down the hallway.

I look at the two outfits carefully laid out on my bed for the fiftieth time this morning. I can't decide what to wear. I have the still-new turquoise spaghetti strap sundress that looks really cute on me but that I never managed to wear all summer. I just didn't have anywhere to wear it. Or I have my new "Go Green" T-shirt and recycled jeans. The dress says I had a great summer and don't want it to end. But the eco-friendly outfit makes a statement and shows I'm environmentally aware. Of course, the dress might make people think I'm trying too hard. Which I obviously am. Then again, so might the green outfit. Argh! This is hard. I've never had to pick out the all-important first day of school outfit on my own before. Sienna and I always had our outfits down weeks beforehand.

"You're still not dressed?" Mom asks, appearing in my doorway. She's already in a silk top and a skirt, ready for work.

"I will be. Just a sec."

"Seriously, Tori, you've got five minutes and then you're busing it."

"Okay, okay," I say, shutting the door. I grab the green outfit and change quickly. The sundress would have been a lie anyway. The summer totally blew. And it's all Sienna's fault.

I check my reflection in the mirror and give my mostly straight brown hair one final brush. I can't help, for the thousandth time this summer, thinking about Sienna. Why hasn't she called me? Or e-mailed? Texted? Anything? We've been best friends since kindergarten and it was bad enough that I had to endure the entire summer without her while she and her family were in Florida. Torturous, really. But what is with the silent treatment these last six weeks? She didn't have a single minute to send one lousy postcard? I know that she's rich and all now, but that's even more reason for her to send me a postcard. Make that a hundred postcards.

Sea started out the summer e-mailing me every day—long e-mails detailing everything from the starfish she saw swept up on the beach to the seagull that pooped on the front window of their rental car. Then the e-mails started tapering off, getting shorter and shorter and farther in between. I kept writing, of course, even though she never answered any of my questions or commented on what was going on in my life. The last e-mail I got was six weeks ago and it only said, "I'm getting ready to go out for dinner." That's it. Nothing more. If I was more paranoid I'd think some bad guys kidnapped her entire family at an all-you-can-eat seafood buffet and she's locked in a dingy basement somewhere without wireless access. I'm not paranoid though, so the only other thing that could have happened is Sea is ignoring me. But why?

"I'll be in the car," Mom yells, and I hear the front door slam shut.

"I'm coming," I holler back, but of course she can't hear me. I slip my backpack over my shoulders and race for the door, only stopping briefly to grab a strawberry fruit bar from the pantry.

Mom is tapping her fingers impatiently on the steering wheel when I climb in. "Sorry, Mom," I say. The car smells overwhelmingly peachy from the candle-shaped air freshener she has hanging from the rearview mirror.

Mom takes a deep breath through her nose. "No, I'm sorry, sweets. It's just I have this really important meeting in fifteen minutes and I can't be late. But it's your first day. Are you excited? Need money?" She plucks a ten from her purse and hands it to me while reversing out of the driveway and into traffic. Mom's a multitasking goddess.

"Thanks." I take the money and tuck it into the front pocket of my backpack. I stare out the window, watching the passing oak trees and street signs with the names of various presidents. We're both silent for a few blocks.

"Nervous?" Mom asks. She's steering with her knees. I hate when she does this. Nine and three, *nine and three*, I always want to say. I'm only twelve and even *I* know you're supposed to keep your hands at nine and three on the steering wheel. Mom pulls a bottle of hand lotion out of the center console, squirts some into her palm, and rubs her hands together. More peach. I don't like peaches.

I shrug.

"It'll be great, honey. Promise." She returns one hand to the steering wheel and dives back into her purse with the other, searching for something.

"Uh-huh," I reply. She says the same thing every year on the first day of school and it's never reached "great" yet. But it's usually been tolerable since Sienna and I have always faced school together. But I don't know about this year. Are we even friends anymore? Did I do something? Does she hate me now? If she does, she could've at least let me know. It's completely unfair to just hate a person and not tell her.

Last year on the first day of school, Sea came to my house at 6:30 in the morning in her pj's, toting her clothes in a duffel bag. Our moms thought we were being silly, but we were determined to get dressed for school together. We both wore jeans but I wore a pretty mint green peasant top and Sea wore a white, fitted tuxedo shirt, complete with the old-fashioned ruffles down the middle. We looked *really* good.

It was a last-minute decision to do our nails in the vampy black polish I'd picked up while shopping with Mom for back-to-school supplies. Sea said it was very *Teen Vogue* and would be the perfect first-day accent.

And it was. For like a minute. But then I got a big glob of vampy black on the right shoulder of my new shirt in an unfortunate hand-waving/nail-blowing incident. Of course Mom chose that precise moment to yell that we had to get in the car *right now*. I looked at Sea, completely freaked. This was the perfect shirt. I didn't have a backup outfit. Sienna didn't panic though. She searched around my desk and then plunged a dry hand into my seashell jewelry box, filled with miscellaneous odds and ends. She pulled out my "Hug a Tree" button and pinned it over the black spot.

"Perfect," she said. But I wasn't so sure. I didn't want to look like a big dork with a button on the shoulder of my shirt on the first day of school. My face must have showed this because then Sea dove into my jewelry box again and pulled out a "Save the Whales" button and pinned it on her shirt in the exact same spot. No one said anything to us about our buttons and maybe we both looked dorky but it didn't matter. I remember I felt a million times better because of Sea that day.

Mom pulls into the Norton Junior High School parking lot and I fidget in my seat. I don't want to get out of the car and start the new school year. See the same students again. The same teachers. I just want to go back home where it's safe and hide in my room with a stack of books. It's pretty much what I did all summer and I'm not quite finished yet.

We stop near the main doors and Mom looks at me with a big smile. "Have a great day, hon. And call me as soon as you get home after school, okay? Remember, no Internet while I'm not home."

I nod but don't move.

"C'mon, Tor. It'll be fine," she assures me. "Go find Sienna."

If Sienna is even here, I think. Maybe her dad took all that new money he made in the stock market last spring and decided to buy them a permanent home in the

Keys rather than just summer there. Maybe he bought her a dozen tutors to sit with her poolside and teach her everything. Maybe he sprang to have a superchip containing every bit of information she'd need to know up through high school implanted in her brain so she doesn't even have to go to school anymore. Now *that* would be cool.

"Seriously, Tor. I have five minutes to make my meeting." Mom hands me my backpack and gives my shoulder a nudge.

"Okay, okay." I sigh and get out of the car. I step up onto the sidewalk and watch my mom pull away from the curb, waving. But I don't wave back. She isn't looking at me anyway.

I remember the day Sienna found out she was loaded like it was yesterday. We were sitting at her kitchen table, cutting pictures of Zane Stewart, the hottie lead singer of the Green Beans, out of magazines to make a collage. Her mom was scrubbing at a scraped-up baker's rack and mumbling curse words about the quality of fiberboard furniture these days. Her dad, whom I've only ever seen on weekends because of his long work hours during the week, came swooping in with a fancy-looking bottle of champagne. He yelled a bunch of stuff about being rich, swung his wife around in a circle, and picked up Sea like she was still five years old.

Everybody was really happy. And I was happy for them too, of course. Sea said nothing would really change. They wouldn't move to a fancy house and she wouldn't transfer to a fancy school. And I'm not saying she lied or anything, but maybe she just didn't know that things would change.

I smooth my T-shirt over my hips and cross my arms over my chest. I look around the courtyard, which is swarming with perky, excited students. No one wants to go into school yet. Everyone's too busy checking out each other's new cell phones and iPods. Both of which are banned inside school. I glance from group to group—the mini fashionistas, the mathletes, the band kids—trying to decide where to go stand until first bell, when my eyes fall on a group of girls huddled around someone. Probably an eighth grader showing off her new designer purse. I'm about to turn away and check the side of the school building when I hear her laugh. Sienna.

My heart beats faster and I'm filled with relief. Thank God she's here. I was really starting to think I'd be doing seventh grade without her. I run for the group of girls. "Sea!" I yell, nudging past a few of them.

Long, beautifully highlighted, low-lighted, flat-ironed hair swooshes in front of me as she turns and we come face-to-face.

I scrunch up my face and peer into her eyes. "Si-enna?" I ask.

She laughs. "Tori! Oh, Tori, I missed you." She throws her tanned arms around my neck and squeezes hard. I peer down at her right shoulder near my cheek. How is she tan? In the seven years I've known Sienna she's never done more than burn in the sun. Is it makeup or something? I rub my fingers on her shoulder and then look at them. Nope. Nothing came off. And that hair?

"Your hair . . ." I begin, pulling back from her embrace.

She laughs again. "You like?" She shakes her head, and her long blond hair glistens in the sun.

"Yeah. I love. But it was short, brown, and curly in May. How'd you do this?" *And why didn't you mention it in one of your e-mails?*

She leans close and whispers in my ear, "Exten-sions."

"Oh," I say, but still don't quite understand. The only extension I've ever had was when I needed extra time on a homework assignment. But her hair looks so real. I reach out to touch it and she laughs and moves away before I do.

"So how was your summer?" she asks.

A wave of emotions washes over me. Part anger at Sea

for dropping off the face of the earth in July, and part relief that she's actually here. She looks at me, waiting for an answer. "Well, uh . . . great," I say, suddenly very self-conscious. There are all these girls still standing around us, listening to every word we say. We're not even friends with most of these girls. Heck, I don't think we've ever even talked to half of them before. They were always "too good" to associate with us. Not that we needed them or anything; Sea and I always had each other.

I want to ask what happened—why she stopped writing me. But I don't want to put her on the defensive by attacking her the first minute I talk to her. "And you?" I ask, bracing myself for the What I Did on My Summer Vacation essay to end all essays.

Sienna giggles. "Oh my god, Tori, it was *so* fabulous. I have to tell you all about it."

Nice. Now she wants to tell me about it. I nod but I'm starting to get weirded out. The other girls still haven't left and in fact are staring at Sienna with big eyes and bigger smiles. Like she's a celebrity or something. And granted, she does look nice. She's got on a super cute navy blue baby-doll dress and she's tan everywhere —down to her perfectly pedicured toes. And dang, she's got on three-inch wedge sandals. For school. My mom still won't let me wear one-inch heels to weddings.

"To start with, the house we stayed in had eighteen bedrooms. Eighteen! I had three to myself alone. And it was right on the beach. I could open my patio doors and walk down to the water, day or night." Hmm. I already know all of this. Sienna described the house in full detail—down to the bidet with the brass angel knob in her personal bathroom—in her very first vacation e-mail. I'm starting to feel like I'm in a play, only I wasn't provided with a script. She closes her eyes and sniffs the air. I take a quick sniff too. What is she smelling? Did the wind shift and we're getting the sewage plant breeze again? She opens her eyes and looks at me. "Sometimes I can almost still smell the ocean air," she adds.

Oh. Ocean air. Right. "Wow. Well, it sounds amazing," I say, hoping my intense jealousy won't leak out all over the place and make a mess.

Sienna nods. "Daddy rented a yacht for the entire summer too and he even let me drive it a couple of times. When we were far from shore, of course."

"Of course," I agree. Like I know. My dad still won't let me drive the grocery cart when we're shopping.

"And then—" she starts but is interrupted by Justin Timberlake. One of his songs, anyway. "Oh, hold on." She slips one hand into a large leather purse, pulls out a pink-sleeved iPhone, and holds it to her ear. "Hello?"

she says and then instantly dissolves into giggles. "Oh, hi, Antonio."

Antonio? That's a boy's name, right? So, there's a boy named Antonio calling her.

Who is this girl and what did she do with my best friend?